Angie swallowed past a suddenly dry throat. There, she'd said the word. "We've developed an unquenchable lust for each other, Finn. So maybe what we should do is ..." Picking her way through verbal land mines, she finished up in a rush. "Maybe the best thing for both of us would be to just get it over with."

Finn spun around to stare at her, and his mouth fell open as she watched. And then he began to laugh— loud, hard guffaws that shattered the stillness of the room.

"You're priceless," he said when he collected himself enough to talk.

Angie felt her cheeks suffuse with warmth. She held her tongue to hide her acute embarrassment.

"I have one more thing to say, Angie."

She looked up. "Well?"

"If and when we make love, it won't be to get it over with."

ABOUT THE AUTHOR

Julie Kistler calls herself "a hardheaded realist with the soul of a romantic." She believes it takes a curious mix of discipline and creativity to think up new, fresh characters and plots, to actually finish what you've started and then send it off into the world. Julie lives in Illinois with her husband, and is now writing full-time.

Books by Julie Kistler

HARLEQUIN AMERICAN ROMANCE

Don't miss any of our special offers. Write to us at the following address for information on our newest releases.

Harlequin Reader Service
P.O. Box 1397, Buffalo, NY 14240
Canadian address: P.O. Box 603,
Fort Erie, Ont. L2A 5X3

JULIE KISTLER

FINN'S ANGEL

Harlequin Books

TORONTO • NEW YORK • LONDON
AMSTERDAM • PARIS • SYDNEY • HAMBURG
STOCKHOLM • ATHENS • TOKYO • MILAN
MADRID • WARSAW • BUDAPEST • AUCKLAND

Published January 1993

ISBN 0-373-16471-8

FINN'S ANGEL

Chapter One

The hair on the back of her neck began to prickle as she pulled her car into its spot in the deserted parking garage.

Something was wrong here. She could feel it.

Without unlocking her door, she twisted in the seat and peered around into the dim recesses of Lot H of the government employees' garage. There were plenty of shadows. But was that all? Or was there someone there, lurking?

"Calm down, Angie," she muttered. "You park in the same place every day, and you know there's nothing out there."

Casting a jaded eye at the expensive automobiles parked cheek-to-jowl with her own, she added caustically, "Nothing except for too many BMWs and Mercedes, when everybody knows public servants ought to be driving inexpensive cars."

Slowly, she eased open the door of her own modest car, catching her briefcase from the passenger seat and swinging her legs out over the concrete floor, careful not to expose too much leg under the tight skirt of her gray wool suit. Of course, there would be no one to see it if she did flash a little thigh, but Angie Marie Boone believed in playing it safe.

The click-clack of her high heels echoed in the gloomy stillness, adding to her anxiety. She just couldn't shake the feeling that something was wrong.

She told herself that the garage seemed scary because it was empty, and that was her own fault, for being so late. On normal days, when she arrived with the rest of the bureaucrats, there were always reassuring clusters of people. But today she'd scheduled a big showdown with her boss, a boss who ranked right up there with Bonnie and Clyde on the Integrity Meter, and she'd had no desire to get to work on time. So she shouldn't be surprised to be all alone in the gloomy parking garage.

"Just nerves," she whispered, but her eyes scanned and rescanned the rows of empty cars, checking for any flicker of movement that might betray the presence of a stranger.

Her nerves had been on red alert for weeks, ever since she'd first begun to suspect that things were not what they seemed at work, in the impressive Department of Housing Affairs. And once she knew for sure what was happening, red alert turned into flaming-scarlet-triple-duty alert, ready to blow off the roof at any moment.

But nobody else knew anything was wrong yet— nobody except for her and the undersecretary himself, Lance Hocker. Lance might be her boss, and he might be a double-dealing skunk of a rat fink, but he was hardly the type to be lurking in parking garages, risking dust streaks on his immaculate Italian suits.

So why did she feel such a sense of foreboding?

Chill out, she ordered herself. But then, in the periphery of her vision, she caught a funny-looking shadow behind a nearby concrete pillar. She stilled. The click-clack of her heels echoed away into nothing.

And the shadow moved.

"Who's there?" she shouted.

Her heart hammered as she brandished her briefcase in front of her, ignoring the fact that the sight of a mere briefcase was unlikely to scare anyone away.

"Angie, it's just me." Gretchen, her best friend at work, offered a weak smile as she edged out from behind the pillar.

Angie put a hand to her chest, willing her heart to find a less painful rhythm. "What are you doing? You scared me half to death!"

Small, plump Gretchen shrugged sheepishly, barely lifting her shoulders inside the heavy fur coat she was wearing. "Sorry. I was waiting for you."

"But why? And why are you wearing that coat?"

Angie peered at her friend. Sharing everything from humble Midwest origins to high career ambitions, they'd hit it off immediately when they'd started work at the DHA. In fact, of all the people Angie knew in Washington, she'd have guessed she knew Gretchen the best.

But she'd never seen her friend wear anything remotely like the opulent fox jacket she was wrapped in today. Aside from the fact that it wasn't her style, it was much too big for her, giving her the appearance of a dwarfed Abominable Snowman.

"Wearing it seemed the easiest way to get it over here from the office," Gretchen explained innocently, waving a hand well-buried inside a furry sleeve. "I brought it along for you—I thought you might need it."

"What?" None of this made any sense, with Gretchen lurking in the parking garage like Deep Throat.

"I have to start at the beginning," Gretchen said hastily. She divested herself of the fox jacket, handing it and an expensive alligator shoulder bag over to Angie. "It all started this morning, when you were late. It's not like you to be late."

"I have an important lunch meeting with Lance Hocker." Angie glanced at her watch. Barely eleven. But even the thought of the upcoming showdown made her feel queasy. "I decided to come in late instead of hanging around all morning, sweating out the minutes."

"You might as well forget about the meeting."

Angie shook her head. "I can't. It's important."

"But—"

"No, Gretchen, I have to be there. I haven't said anything—not even to you—but I've been having some problems with Lance, and he promised to straighten everything out today, at this meeting." She set her jaw firmly. "One way or the other, this whole mess is going to be over with. I have to be there."

"But that's what I've been trying to tell you! You can't meet with Lance, because he took off, vamoose, gone with the wind!"

"Gone? Gone for the day, you mean? Where did he go?"

"Not for the day," Gretchen said impatiently. "For good. And if I knew where, I could sell it to the tabloids for a million bucks."

"I don't get this." Angie tried to juggle the stupid fox coat and the extra purse as she advanced on her friend. "What do you mean, he's gone? He can't be gone! He was supposed to meet with me this morning and explain what the hell has been going on in the department for the last six months. He can't just waltz out with all that money...."

She broke off abruptly as the truth sank in.

"That's it," she whispered. "He only set up the meeting to stall me, to give him time to get out of town. He never intended to make things right."

"I get it," Gretchen returned eagerly. "He took off *because* of your meeting, right? You had the goods on him, so he lit out before you could blow the whistle."

"Oh, my God." Angie dropped the fur, the extra purse, her own purse and her briefcase as she sagged against a parked car.

Wide-eyed, Gretchen joined her, hitching her small, smartly suited body onto a convenient car hood. "Angie, you wouldn't believe the rumors flying at the office. You aren't involved, are you?"

"I helped him," she said miserably. "I was a complete idiot."

"I was afraid of that when I found the fur coat," Gretchen said grimly. "So what did he do? And why on earth did you help?"

Angie looked at the pile of fur dumped in front of her. "What are you talking about? What does the coat have to do with anything?"

"You," Gretchen said logically. "And Lance. I mean, a fur coat positively *reeks* of something Lance would give one of his bimbos. And it's certainly not like you to own something as conspicuous as that thing—or that awful alligator purse, either, for that matter." She frowned. "When I found them in your closet—the one between your office and Lance's—for the first time, I thought maybe the stories were true about you and Lance."

"Stories?" Angie asked with a sense of dread. "What stories are you talking about?"

But Gretchen ignored the question. "I asked myself, how else could Angie afford a fur coat, if it wasn't that creep Lance who gave it to her?" She shook her head sadly. "With all those FBI guys nosing around Lance's office, it would only be a matter of time before they found the closet *and* your stuff. I knew that coat and purse would look bad for you—so I had to get them out of there before the feds got them. Because even if you did help Lance, I know you didn't do it on purpose, and I swear, Angie, I would never turn you over to the FBI. But you never should've taken a fur coat from him. It looks *bad*."

Angie's head was spinning. "But it's not my fur," she protested. "Or my purse! And what do you mean, FBI guys were in Lance's office?"

"Why do you think I'm here, warning you not to go into the office?" Gretchen glanced around nervously before continuing. "That's the whole thing, Angie. When I got to work this morning, I went by your office to see if you wanted to go for coffee. Well, of course you weren't there. But right next door, outside Lance's office, the place was swarming with feds, state cops and a few ugly types I don't think have anything to do with the legal side of the action, if you get my drift."

"Like gangsters? Is that what you're saying?"

"Exactly," Gretchen said in a heated tone. "And all of them were having fits that Lance was nowhere to be found. I told you, there are rumors all over the place—that you and Lance ran off together, or that he sold secrets to a foreign country, or..."

"We work in the housing department," Angie reminded her friend. "What kind of *housing* secrets are there to sell?"

"I don't know, but it had to be something good for this big a bust."

"Oh, it's good," Angie murmured, sweeping a stray tendril of brown hair back from her forehead. Even her usually tidy bun, always twisted perfectly at the nape of her neck, was falling apart. "Let's just say Lance was making a bundle by stealing from the poor and giving to himself."

"Kickbacks, you mean? Or what?"

"A little bit of everything, I think." Wearily, she laid out the facts. "The way I've pieced it together, our dear boss Lance accepted housing project bids that were way too low, from some very suspicious contractors—the kind whose buildings fall down if you look at them funny."

"Crooks, huh? And they paid him off?"

"I don't know." She added, "But I do know he doctored the figures to make the bids look okay, and then I think he pocketed the difference."

"What a scum," Gretchen muttered.

"A stupid scum," Angie returned. "I think he was cheating both the taxpayers *and* his partners. I caught a phone call from one of them a few weeks ago. This guy sounded like the thug type. He left a message for Lance—something like 'Pay up or you're dead meat.' I knew it was weird, but I didn't exactly know what to do."

"But you said you helped him," Gretchen reminded her. "What did you mean? You didn't really help him, did you?"

"Not in the way you mean. All I really did was not tell anybody but him what I suspected. But I didn't realize he would run. I thought he was...telling the truth," she finished lamely.

"Lance Hocker? Tell the truth? Are you crazy?"

She tried to explain, but she wasn't sure she understood herself. "I didn't really have anything on him, except for a set of low bids that were suspicious, but not exactly *criminal*. I asked him about them, and he said it was just a mistake. So I let him..." She sighed. "I let him change the numbers."

"You what?"

"Well, he seemed sincere at the time—about wanting to fix his mistake, so I...well, I let him."

Gretchen practically fell down in her obvious shock. "You had Lance Hocker dead to rights and you let him off the hook? Are you crazy?"

"I'm beginning to think so," Angie muttered as Gretchen continued her diatribe.

"Lance Hocker is a scum-bucket, a lowlife, a career politician with the morals of a maggot." Gretchen threw up her hands. "Finally, he goes too far—you catch him in the act of changing bids, which is enough to get him kicked out right there, and you let him *walk?*"

"I didn't know!" she protested.

"But Angie, you did know! You knew he was stealing money big-time, and you didn't tell anyone. Why not?"

"I already told you—he asked for time to fix things." Angie turned mournful eyes to her friend. "He told me it was all a mistake, and that his career would be ruined, so if I had any ethics, any professional scruples, I wouldn't say anything."

"And you bought that?"

"Lance can be very persuasive when he wants to, you know. And I couldn't see what it would hurt to wait a few weeks, until he could make amends."

"Angie!"

"I know, I know. But remember, at that point, I didn't really know what was going on." Shaking her head, she said softly, "And Lance said that no one would ever have to know, that the department's reputation wouldn't have to suffer, and all our jobs would be safe. I guess I thought that was worth a few weeks."

"So you gave him the time he asked for...."

"And he flew the coop."

There was a long, depressing pause. "What are you going to do?"

Angie stood up, squaring her shoulders. "I'm going to walk into my office and confront the feds. I don't have anything to hide. I mean, I guess I was sort of an accessory, but that was an honest mistake, so—"

"Umm, Angie?"

"What?"

"You might want to rethink that."

She glanced over at Gretchen's stricken face. "Why?"

"Do you remember I told you there were rumors about you and Lance?"

"Well, yes, but people always talk. So what?"

Reluctantly, Gretchen announced, "A lot of people on staff think that you two were having this torrid affair, and that you seduced him into the criminal stuff."

"Me?" All her life she'd been the Goody Two-shoes whom nobody ever suspected of anything. Why did people have to cast her as Mata Hari now? "A torrid affair? Is this a joke?"

"Sandy in the steno pool and Marcus from PR both said Lance had been bragging about what a hot thing the two of you had going on—for a couple of weeks now."

"But what about the Contessa?"

"The who?"

"The Contessa," Angie repeated grimly. "Contessa Bibi von Kronenburg. The blond bimbo whose picture is always in the newspaper. The woman he's been dating—if you want to call that *dating*. I caught him with her a couple of times when I worked late, and they were all over each other. And she definitely came last, if we're keeping his torrid affairs in chronological order. So why doesn't anyone suspect *her* of being in on his scam?''

''I guess no one knows about her.'' Gretchen reflected for a moment. ''Although I don't know how he could keep her a secret. I mean, I've seen her picture. She may be a bimbo, but she's also fabulous-looking. Especially with all that hair.''

''Yeah, it's her trademark,'' Angie said morosely. ''All frizzed out like that—we used to call it angel hair.''

''Well, Bibi doesn't look like any angel to me. Not with the clothes she wears.'' Gretchen shook her head. ''She's gorgeous, not to mention filthy rich. What would she want with Lance?''

''He has lots of money, too,'' Angie offered dryly. ''The taxpayers' money.''

''Bibi von Kronenburg. Wow. That's the big leagues.''

Angie stooped and poked at the pile of fox fur she'd dropped on the dusty concrete. Dangling the alligator bag over one arm, she remarked, ''I'm betting both of these are hers, too. She probably left them behind after some scummy little tryst with Lance.''

''I'm sorry, Angie.'' Gretchen gave her a sheepish look. ''About the fur, I mean. Since they were in the closet you shared with Lance, I assumed they were yours. And I thought you might need them if you were going on the lam.''

"On the lam," she echoed mournfully. It sounded like a gangster movie. But then, so did her whole life at the moment. "I tried to be so professional, to do the right thing, and he told people I was a criminal or something."

"He did more than that."

Angie sat back on the car hood with a thump. "What do you mean?"

"He left stuff in the office. Stuff that apparently points the finger at you."

"But how...?"

"I don't really know." Gretchen reached out helplessly, patting Angie's arm. "I'm really sorry. Everyone was talking about it, floating theories about you and Lance and this hot criminal love affair."

"But you came out here—"

"Well, I didn't believe for a minute that you ran off with that creep, and I sure didn't believe that whatever trouble Lance was in was your fault. But one of the FBI agents was looking for you and asking a lot of questions, and he made it sound like you were in it up to your hips. So I thought I'd run out here and head you off."

"Oh, brother. How am I going to explain this to the FBI?" Angie asked anxiously. "Or to anybody?"

"Angie!" Gretchen exclaimed. "You can't talk to them! They'll throw you in jail, or worse."

"But—"

"Listen, Angie, you're in a lot of trouble. You and I both know that Lance Hocker is capable of just about anything to save his own hide, and it sounds like he decided you'd make a dandy fall guy for him and this Bibi chick."

Oh, that did sound like Lance. It sounded so perfectly like him, Angie thought she might scream.

"And those huge men who were hanging around the building..." Gretchen shuddered. "I wouldn't want those apes on my trail."

"On my trail?" she whispered.

"The FBI, the cops, the gangsters—they were all asking about you."

Her eyes found her friend's face. "And now everyone thinks I...?"

"Masterminded the whole thing." Gretchen crossed her arms over her chest. "Meanwhile, Lance is probably on some tropical beach, oiling the nubile body of that bimbo even as we speak."

Angie's head began to swim. "What am I going to do?"

"You could hide out at my place...." Gretchen said dubiously.

"Gretchen, I couldn't do that—then you'd be in trouble, too. Besides, it's the first place they'd look." She saw relief pass quickly over her friend's face, and she knew she'd said the right thing. "No, I think the best thing I can do right now is get out of town— somewhere nobody will find me."

"Out of town?" Gretchen echoed. "Like where?"

"Somewhere far, far away," she said with satisfaction. "It doesn't matter where, as long as it's not here. And while I'm lying low, maybe the stupid cops will trip over Lance and Bibi and let me off the hook."

"I guess that sounds okay, Angie. But where will you go?"

Angie chewed her lip. "That's the problem. I mean, there's my parents' farm in Nebraska, but I hate Nebraska, and I hate farms. And I'm not that crazy about my parents, for that matter."

"You can't go to your parents. If my apartment is first, your parents' house is the second place they'll look."

"Then where?" Angie paced off a small space on the cold concrete as she considered. "What do real criminals do when they want to disappear? There must be ways to do this sort of thing."

Gretchen offered hopefully, "I saw this guy on 'America's Most Wanted' who'd disappeared, and he wasn't found for forty years."

"I saw that, too. All he did was disguise himself with glasses and a mustache, and nobody recognized him."

"So you could get glasses. I mean, the mustache is out, but—"

"That's it, don't you see?" Angie began to pick up steam. "Not a mustache or glasses, but just to change the way I look. I could dye my hair, wear different clothes—no one would know it was me." Lifting a loose tendril, she contemplated the idea. Fire-engine red, Elvira black, even platinum blond—anything was possible. "It might actually be fun," she announced with determination.

"Sure," Gretchen said gloomily. "Fun. Besides, what choice do you have?"

She couldn't think of one. "Okay, so I'm doing the disguise thing. But I still haven't figured out where to go." She shook her head. The more she thought about this, the more tangled it became. "And then there's the money problem."

"What money problem?"

"The problem of how I pay for my little disappearing act." Angie sat back down on the car next to Gretchen. "I barely have enough for bus fare in my purse, and I'm not sure I dare go back home or to the bank." She wondered if she was getting paranoid. No, it wasn't paranoia if people really were out to get her. And they were. "If they're waiting for me at work, then I'm sure my apartment is being staked out. I can't go home. And I can't use my automatic teller card, because they'd probably send cops to the machine before they'd let my money go."

"You're right." Gretchen seemed to be having difficulty spitting something out. "Angie . . . ?"

"What?"

"The purse? The contessa's purse?"

She was too busy trying to figure out a way to save her skin to worry about dopey Contessa Bibi and her damned alligator bag. "What about it?"

"Well, I sort of glanced inside it on the way over here. I'm sorry—I know that's really awful of me, to look inside your purse. Well, now I know it's not your purse, but then I thought it was. So, anyway, the thing is . . ."

"What? The thing is, what?"

"The thing is, it's full of money," Gretchen said delicately. "A big pile of twenties."

Desperately, Angie flipped open the top of the purse and pulled out the wad of bills, doing quick calculations as she thumbed the stack. "Good Lord." Her eyes flashed up to Gretchen. "There's eight or nine hundred dollars here. You don't suppose it's counterfeit, do you?"

"Why would it be?"

"Add that to Lance's other crimes, I suppose." Angie sifted through the pile of twenties. "But no, I think they're real. It's just like Contessa Bibi to be tooling around with almost a thousand bucks in her purse."

"Are you going to keep it?"

Snapping the purse shut, Angie smiled. "You bet I am. It's almost like justice, don't you think? Those two idiots ran away, leaving me to be the patsy, to take the fall. And now her money gives me a way to escape."

"So you're really going to run?"

Angie held her breath for a long moment. She considered every angle of her situation, and she hated what she saw. She had never been a quitter or a coward, but she knew she was no match for the combined forces of the United States government and every hit man in the free world.

If she stayed, she'd end up in prison or dead. It was as simple as that.

"You have to promise me you won't say a word to anyone," she said slowly. "You never saw me this morning, okay?"

Gretchen swallowed. Her eyes were wide when she answered, "I swear, Angie. Not even a word."

"Okay then."

"So you're going?"

"Maybe on the train." Angie smiled. "I always liked trains."

Chapter Two

This had to be the oddest day she'd ever spent. But the weird thing was, she was sort of enjoying herself.

Once she got used to the idea that everything she'd worked and planned for career-wise was down the toilet, that life as she knew it had ceased to exist, what was left but to throw caution to the winds and enjoy playing Secret Agent Girl?

First she'd driven her car to the airport, and then wasted several long moments trying to say goodbye to it. She reminded herself that hard-boiled criminals on the lam could not afford to get sentimental about their vehicles, so she forced herself to abandon her little Chevy in the airport parking lot without a backward glance.

Somebody will find it, she told herself bravely. Hopefully, the poor little thing wouldn't have to sit out in the cold all by itself for too long.

Then she rented a locker inside the airport, dumping her briefcase, her suit jacket, her trademark pearls and most of her IDs and credit cards. Although she fought with herself over it for quite a while, she still couldn't bear to give up her platinum American Express card. She'd been so happy when it came in the mail a few weeks ago, seeing the small square of plastic as a symbol of all she'd hoped to achieve when she came to Washington. How could she give it up now?

Poking it down into the recesses of Contessa Bibi's alligator purse, Angie promised herself she wouldn't use the card except in an extreme emergency.

Too bad Bibi hadn't left her own credit cards. Then at least Angie could've rented a car to skip town in. But the alligator bag yielded only an expired passport from Ruritania, wherever the heck that was, an international driver's license and the wad of bills. That meant commuter trains and buses to get around town, but it would have to do.

After letting her hair down from its bun and hiding inside the fox jacket, she felt sufficiently disguised to take the next step.

The mall.

Methodically, she haunted the aisles at a department store, finally choosing a large nylon duffel bag, a few items of casual clothing, some flat suede boots, and then the absolute essentials like deodorant and toothpaste. Intent on her task, she felt like a hired killer in a spy movie. Hastily, she donned the new clothes in the store's rest room, stuffed her career-girl togs and the rest of the items in the duffel bag, and then hurried along to her next stop.

The beauty parlor.

To complete her new look, she purposely chose the busiest place she could think of, a psychedelic little salon called Hair and Now, where all the teens hung out.

"I have a picture," Angie said weakly, handing over Bibi's passport photo to the hairdresser. "Can you do this?"

"Yeah, sure," the stylist muttered. "Kim Basinger number four—the curly one."

Angie took a deep breath, cast a fond look in the mirror at her plain, straight-as-a-board, medium-brown hair, and kissed the last traces of Angie Marie Boone goodbye.

It took hours to get what she wanted. Her nerves were escalating to the edge of panic as she began to feel sure that the FBI or even the gangsters could've located her by now. But finally, blessedly, the rods were removed, the dye was rinsed out, she was shampooed and conditioned and blow-dried, and left...speechless.

The stylist spun Angie in the chair, sending a curtain of exotic blond hair flying. "So, way cool, huh? Kinda retro. Totally excellent."

"Well, it's different."

"Ordinary, you can go, like, somewhere else. Different, we do here."

Limply, Angie lifted an endless strand of crimped, white-blond hair. She had never seen herself with so much hair—let alone this amazing color—and frizzed out like a Christmas angel on drugs. But she had to admit, it was eye-catching, and not that different from the bountiful blond mane of Contessa Bibi the bimbo. The idea was not only to resemble Bibi enough to use her IDs if necessary, but also to create a distraction. If the sheer volume of her hair was this overwhelming, hopefully no one would notice who was hiding underneath.

But when it came time to pay for this masterpiece, she was less sure she'd done the right thing.

"How much?" she asked around the obstruction in her throat.

"Only a hundred and forty-five," the girl repeated glumly. "We're having a special."

"Right." She peeled off the bills with a sense of dread. Already she'd spent almost four hundred of her precious dollars, and she hadn't even gotten to the train station yet. By the time she got to wherever she was going, she'd be down to nickels and dimes.

Angie folded her wallet and stuck it back in Bibi's alligator bag. Time to get this show on the road. As far as she was concerned, she couldn't get out of Washington, D.C., fast enough.

THE MAN SITTING ACROSS from her was reading the *New York Post*. And her face was plastered all over the front of it.

Angie hid behind her mountain of hair, forcing herself to look away from the paper and out the window into the rapidly darkening countryside. Where the heck were they? Ohio? Or Indiana, maybe. The train just kept rattling on, packed to the gills, while the man across from her held up her face for all the world to see.

She couldn't help it; she had to know what it said. Surreptitiously, she sneaked a look back in that direction.

Politico's Sex Kitten! the paper shouted, with a splash of bold letters blazoned under her picture. It was a lousy picture, too, the one she'd had taken for her federal employee security badge, with flat brown hair pulled straight back from an unsmiling face. It looked like a mug shot. Maybe that was prophetic, after all.

She peered at the newspaper, trying to make out more of the story.

Scandal broadens as the search for the bureaucrat and his illicit paramour intensifies. Housing undersecretary Lance Hocker and his mistress, Angie Marie Boone, have vanished. Sources close to Hocker indicate that Boone was pressuring her lover to run away with her to conceal the theft of millions of dollars that she'd embezzled.

She didn't know which was worse, being suspected of stealing millions of dollars of the taxpayers' money, or being accused of being Lance's "sex kitten" on the front page of every paper in the country.

The woman next to her, a cozy grandma type, nodded at Angie to indicate that she, too, was interested in the story. Angie tried to look nonchalant, to hide once again behind the long fall of blond waves, but she felt like an idiot. All this hair made her feel obvious and silly, as if she were angling for attention, not trying to lie low.

"Isn't it terrible?" the woman offered confidentially. She pointed at the newspaper. "They say that girl ran off with zillions, and maybe even killed her boss, because he knew what she did. They're all looking for her, but *I* know where she is."

"You do?" Angie asked weakly.

The woman nodded. "Cuba," she whispered.

"Cuba?" Trying not to expire with relief, she couldn't help asking, "Why Cuba?"

"Because those communists don't care if she is a murderer, that's why."

"Oh, I see," she murmured, as if it all made perfect sense. One thing was certain—if everybody else was as loony as this lady, Angie would be safe for a good, long time. Next they'd be saying she'd been spotted cavorting with Elvis in the Bermuda Triangle.

She had to admit, she felt a certain amount of perverse satisfaction, sitting there as big as life while everyone ran around in circles searching for her. But people expected Angie Marie Boone, master criminal, to have straight brown hair, carefully pulled back in a knot. They expected her to be in a classy suit, with a discreetly cut silk blouse and one strand of perfect pearls. It was the way she'd always dressed for work, the way she'd wanted the people at the undersecretary's office to picture her. She was Angie Boone, up-and-comer, the one person on staff with everything on the ball.

So it shouldn't be surprising that she was going unrecognized, sitting here with oodles of pale blond hair and a dippy fox fur jacket. She looked like she was on her way to audition for a C-grade movie, not to hide from the law.

"Are you an actress, dear?" the woman inquired, echoing Angie's own thoughts.

"Uh, no, I'm not. Why do you ask?"

"I just had a feeling." She smiled pleasantly. "When I get these feelings, I'm always right. Perhaps you're not an actress now, but you will be. Or maybe you were in a previous life. But I'm getting these very strong vibrations, something about disguises and false faces. Are you sure you've never been an actress?"

"No, never." Even as she denied it, Angie began to feel very uncomfortable. The lady was clearly loose a few screws, but she wasn't all that far from the truth, what with the disguises and the false faces.

"I'm psychic, you see," the woman said cheerfully. "That's how I know about Cuba. You mark my words, they'll find that horrible woman there."

A psychic on one side and a man with a dangerous newspaper directly across. It was going to be a long trip.

"So where are you going, dear?"

"Seattle," Angie said reluctantly. She wasn't sure it was prudent to part with the information, but what could it really hurt? Besides, the woman thought she could read minds. No matter what Angie said, the lady would think she knew where she was going.

Cuba, no doubt, she thought perversely.

"Seattle is lovely," the psychic grandma offered. "Very spiritual. But I don't think that's where you're going."

"Yes, I am," Angie said firmly.

"Oh, you may think you are. But we don't always end up where we think we will."

"I'm going to Seattle."

"Just wait, dear. You'll see."

Luckily, grandma decided to go back to her knitting, leaving Angie free from any more odd-ball prognostications. And when the man across from her fell into an open-mouthed doze, letting his paper fall into a heap in his lap, she actually began to breathe a bit more easily.

No more crazy psychic, no more staring at her own face. Things were looking up. Until the conductor came swinging down the center aisle.

"Another half hour to Chicago," he called out. "If you're switching trains or getting off at Union Station, please make sure you take everything with you."

Angie glanced down at her watch. They'd be early coming into Chicago. Maybe that was a good omen. Everybody knew you were never early traveling by train.

"Sir?" she asked, sitting up straighter and leaning over the knitting lady toward the aisle. "I'm going to Seattle. Do I stay on this train?"

"Yes, ma'am," he said politely. "But you'll probably want to get out and walk around. We'll be in Chicago for a couple of hours."

"A couple of hours?" she echoed.

"Yes, ma'am. We're getting in early, so we'll have to wait for the rest of our cars to catch up. It'll be at least two hours, maybe three. Plenty of time to get out, eat some dinner, buy something to read in one of the shops."

Like a newspaper with her face on it. What a great idea. She was still stewing over the problem of how to spend the extra time when they pulled into Union Station with a high-pitched squealing of brakes and the rustle of tired, cranky passengers.

Grandma began to gather her things before they'd even come to a full stop. "Enjoy your trip," she told Angie kindly. "Wherever you end up."

"Seattle," Angie repeated.

"No, not Seattle," the lady insisted. "Somewhere with corn. I'm sure of it."

Good heavens. That sounded like Nebraska. Maybe Angie was just feeling paranoid, but the one place she would rather die than end up was back home with her parents. She was trying to joke herself out of taking the psychic's prediction seriously when the man across from her roused himself and straightened out his newspaper.

Instead of reading inside, with the front page and her picture facing out, he refolded it and began to peruse page one. He seemed to be spending an inordinate amount of time studying her photo, narrowing his eyes at it as if he thought he knew her.

Angie began to sweat.

"I could swear I've seen this face before," he mumbled.

"Yes, I thought so, too," Grandma put in as she hopped into the aisle with her knitting bag. "I'm hoping there will be more pictures in some of the other newspapers so I can get a better look. Maybe you should look at the other papers, too."

"Good idea." The man with the paper shook his head. "I never forget a face, and I know I've seen this one before."

"Are you getting off here?" Angie asked hopefully. Maybe if she got them talking about something else, they wouldn't realize that the face they recognized had been sharing a train car with them for hundreds of miles.

"Nah," the guy muttered. "Except maybe to get a couple more papers, like the old lady suggested. I'm going all the way to Seattle."

So Mr. "I Never Forget a Face" was going all the way to Seattle with her. What were the chances she could get that far without him making the connection?

"I guess I'll get off and, uh, get something to eat," Angie improvised quickly. All she knew was that she wanted to be far, far away from Granny and the lout with the paper.

Retrieving her duffel bag, she got into the slow line of departing passengers a few people behind Grandma, leaving the newspaper man still sitting on the train. Why couldn't they move more quickly? At this rate, she'd be pinned ten feet from the door when the man realized where he'd seen her. In other words, a sitting duck.

But finally, she saw daylight. As soon as her feet hit the ground, she maneuvered around a clump of people struggling with their luggage, heading for the main part of the station.

Good grief! There were cops everywhere, and they seemed to be scanning the faces of every person who walked by. She pretended to be fascinated by the big tote board of arrivals and departures, which kept her

from having to pass right in front of the nearest po-
liceman.

Think, Angie, she commanded. *What are you going to do?*

And then it came to her. Whatever the next train
was out of this place, she'd be on it. That way she
could duck back into the tunnel where the trains were
without anyone the wiser. She tried to remember to
keep breathing and to act like nothing was wrong as
she glanced over the list of trains. But nothing seemed
to be leaving any time soon.

Except Omaha. She shuddered. No way!

And then her eyes lit on New Orleans. The train was
leaving in six minutes. New Orleans would be lovely
this time of year, not nearly as dark and gloomy as
Seattle. She began to cheer up. Why had she wanted
to go to Seattle, anyway? New Orleans was a much
better choice.

The only problem was that she had a ticket to Seattle, and not enough money to buy a new one. *Too bad!*
she decided, juggling her duffel bag, her hideous fur
and Bibi's purse as she raced down the corridor to the
southbound trains. New Orleans cost less than Seattle, so surely they'd accept her old ticket.

As she settled into her new seat on the practically
empty train, she felt sure she'd done the right thing. It
was dark outside as the train pulled away from Chicago, and all she could see were miles of snow and a
few twinkling lights.

Before she knew it, the steady, rhythmic motion of
the wheels had lulled her into a drowsy, sleepy sense of
security. Newspapers and grandma psychics seemed

very far away as she thought about New Orleans, Cajun food and jazz on Bourbon Street.

Only a few months till Mardi Gras. Maybe she wouldn't be there that long, but you never knew....

"Miss?"

Angie's eyes snapped open. "Hmm?" she managed, pulling herself into a sitting position. How long had she been asleep?

"I need your ticket, miss," the conductor said kindly. "Time to punch the ol' ticket."

"Oh, ticket. Right." She fished it out of her purse and handed it over, hoping for the best.

There was a long pause as he studied the stub. After a moment, he said, "I'm sorry, miss, but you don't have the right ticket."

"I don't?" Maybe if she played dumb, everything would turn out okay.

"Your ticket is to Seattle, miss. This is the train to New Orleans."

"Oh, that's okay. I'd just as soon go to New Orleans."

He shook his head. "I'm sorry, but you'll have to get off at the next stop and buy another ticket if you want to go to New Orleans."

"The next stop? Where are we?"

"Coming in to Champaign, Illinois. We're about a hundred and fifty miles south of Chicago."

"But—" she began to protest, before the conductor cut her off with a stern look.

"I'm sorry, miss, but you got to have the right ticket to ride these rails. Best I can do is let you off in

Champaign. Look at it this way—you got a free ride this far.''

It was small consolation. So there she was, dumped unceremoniously in Champaign—wherever that was—with very little money, no friends and no prospects.

She should've known. Running right along with her luck so far, the ticket window was already closed for the night. Even if she could've talked them into trading in her ticket, which she realized was unlikely, she wouldn't be doing it tonight.

As the few remaining passengers wandered past her on their way out of the station, Angie cast a suspicious gaze at her unappealing surroundings. The train station was just one big room, with a few uncomfortable-looking benches scattered around.

Had it come to this? Was she going to be spending the night camped out in the train station, like some homeless waif?

''Angel,'' a small voice whispered from down behind her knees. And then someone tugged at her furry sleeve.

Had that tiny voice said *Angie?* It was enough to make her freeze into an icicle of anxiety.

Not now, she pleaded. Not after Lance and Bibi, hairdressers with studs in their noses, crazy fortune-tellers, men with photographic memories... It was too much!

She stood her ground, refusing to turn and confront her accuser until she was forced to, trying not to scream or tear out her bizarre hair.

"Sorry, miss," a deeper, rougher voice said, not sounding the least bit sorry. "He thinks you're an angel. Must be the hair."

"My hair? Oh, he said *angel*." She sagged with relief, turning as she whispered, "I thought he said... Oh."

It was the only word she could think of when she saw the man. He was gorgeous, in a way that was totally out of place in these mundane surroundings. She got an impression of dark hair, left a little too long, light eyes and beautifully chiseled features. He was wearing scuffed cowboy boots, faded, disreputable jeans, an equally scuffed leather jacket and a tough, closed expression.

James Dean in the train station in Champaign, Illinois.

"What are you doing here?" she asked him.

He just watched her, telling her with his icy blue eyes, if not his words, that he didn't answer questions unless he had a damn good reason.

The child at his side reached up to gingerly finger a stray tendril of her wretched angel hair. The boy looked no more than four or five, with scraggly hair and wide, wide eyes. He was staring at her with awe and disbelief.

"Angel," he said again, in that tiny, reverent voice. "Finn, Finn, I foun' an angel. For Christmas."

"Yeah, bucko. She's an angel all right." The man named Finn hoisted the child up into his arms, giving his small friend a smile. "Time to go back home, Derek. You ready to roll?"

"No, no," the boy insisted, beginning to wiggle. "Let's take Angel home. There's room."

"Sorry, pal," the man said softly. "It doesn't work that way. The kid we came for didn't show, so it's just you and me. We don't take substitutes."

"No," Derek said emphatically. "Angel needs to come to our house. We got room, Finn. E'rybody welcome. You say so, Finn. E'rybody can come to our house."

"Derek—" he began, but Angie was getting curious.

"Wait a minute," she put in. "You came to pick up a child who isn't here? Aren't you worried?"

The man studied her for a moment. "Sometimes they're here, sometimes they're not. It's the nature of the business."

What kind of business picked up children in train stations late at night? She wasn't sure she was ready to throw her body in between him and Derek, even if he were some sort of pimp or pervert, but it was worth a try. "What exactly do you mean?" she demanded.

Gently he set Derek back down on the floor and then just stood there, as if deciding whether he wanted to go any further into explanations. "I run a shelter," he said finally. "For runaways."

Angie glanced down at small, innocent Derek. "And this child is a runaway?"

"Sort of." The man shrugged. "Runaway—homeless—it's all the same to me. If they need a place, I take them in."

He certainly didn't look like a social reformer; he wasn't a bit kind or gentle or anything else she would associate with a do-gooder. In fact, he was downright surly. For all she knew, he was on the prowl for fresh meat, and she had Prime Choice stamped on her forehead.

"So you were here to pick up another child for your shelter?" she asked warily.

"Yeah, that's right." And with that chilly, knowing gaze, he looked her up and down twice. "You know, lady, Derek may think you're an angel, but I don't."

"No?"

"Nope. I know exactly what you are."

Exactly? As in, Politico's Sex Kitten? She shivered. "I—I don't know what you mean."

"Sure you do, lady."

"No, really—"

But he cut her off with an impatient wave of one hand. "I know a fake when I see one. That duffel bag is cheap, your clothes are cheap—but your coat looks pretty pricey. My guess is it's not yours. You stole it, didn't you?"

If the worst he thought was that she'd stolen Bibi's tacky fur, she was still safe. "I'm no thief," she said flatly.

"Don't bother to lie. I'm an expert."

She pulled her chin up. "At what exactly are you an expert, Mr . . . ?"

"Sheridan. Finn Sheridan. I'm an expert at spotting liars."

"Liars?"

"And runaways. And that's what you are."

"Which? The liar or the runaway?"

"Both." He paused. "You still want an angel, Derek?"

"Yes," the child said solemnly. "Home. Angel come home."

"Well, she's a little older than the kids I usually take, but I suppose I could make an exception." He smiled then, just barely, softening his lean face enough to hint at a dimple on one side, taking her breath clean away. "So, tell me, Angel, could you do with a bed for the night?"

Chapter Three

There was no answer from the mysterious blonde. And Finn wasn't given to excess patience. "Look, lady, I can offer you shelter if you want, but I'm not hanging out here all night waiting for you to make up your mind. Are you interested or not?"

"I—I don't know."

She licked her lip nervously, and he couldn't keep his eyes off the tiny motion. She had a beautiful, tender mouth, very soft and vulnerable-looking. That mouth was completely at odds with the flashy hairdo and gaudy fur coat. He couldn't help noticing, or wondering about her.

Which was real? Was she the angel those sweet, trembling lips promised? Or the kind of brassy runaway who'd steal a fur coat? He wished he knew. And that was a bad sign—a warning that he should stay as far away from her as possible.

You can take them in, Father Maguire had told him so many times. *The good ones, the bad ones—accept them all with open arms and try to make a difference.*

*But remember, Finn: if you get too involved, you and
your shelter won't last five minutes.*

So much for the sense in asking her home. He was
already beginning to regret his generous impulse.

"Finn, Finn," Derek whispered, tugging on his
sleeve. "Brin' her. Brin' angel wif us, Finn."

"I asked, kid. If the angel doesn't want to come
with us, there's not much I can do."

"You make her," the little boy said logically. "You
bigger 'n her."

"I'm not gonna carry her off," he said dryly. "I
don't think that would go over too well."

"Please, Finn. Please, please, please?"

He was fond of Derek, and God knew, the kid
didn't ask for much. He was trying awfully hard to go
along with Derek's wishes, but it wasn't easy when this
siren in a stolen fur coat was tempting him to run, not
walk, in the opposite direction.

Oh, he'd had tougher customers come through his
place, with equally big chips on their shoulders and
equally defiant gleams in their eyes. But he'd never
taken in anyone as dangerous to his own personal well-
being as this pretty little angel. All of his instincts told
him that she was scared, she was in trouble, and he
couldn't trust her as far as he could throw her. Which
meant she was exactly the kind of woman who got
under his skin.

But he was older and tougher now, immune to
damsels in distress. Or so he told himself. Repeatedly.

"Finn?" Derek pleaded, and Finn knew he couldn't
hold out against that small, desperate face. He'd give
it one more shot. A small one.

"So what's it gonna be?" he asked, trying to maintain a relatively civil air. "The offer's closing quick."

"Well . . . Well, maybe," she said finally. "I mean, if this runaway shelter thing is on the up and up."

Still looking suspicious, she gazed down at Derek and then back up to Finn, scrutinizing them from head to foot, frowning, as if she thought they were both something out of *Oliver Twist*.

"Does the kid look mistreated?" Finn asked sharply.

"No, but—"

He cut her off with a wave of his hand. "If you think I'm running some kind of racket, you can ask a cop."

"Uh, no—"

"Every cop in Champaign knows about my place, because they bring me kids with nowhere else to go. I saw a patrolman I know, right down the block. He was on his way in to dinner when we got here. You want to ask him?"

"No!" she said quickly. Too quickly. But she recovered, offering primly, "That won't be necessary. I believe you, Mr. Sheridan."

Narrowing his eyes, Finn chewed on that bit of information. He'd seen the panic in her eyes when he mentioned the word *cop*, which could only mean that she'd had a run-in with the police and was in no hurry to get caught again. This was just dandy. Not only was she a runaway, but in all likelihood, a criminal to boot.

But Derek was none the wiser, turning shining eyes toward his angel. "Please, Angel," the little boy begged.

"I—I guess so."

"Okay, then let's get out of here." Finn grabbed her duffel bag, hoisted Derek up in his other arm, and strode for the door. But he'd only gone a few steps before he turned back to see if she was following. She was.

He stopped, giving her a chance to catch up. "What's your name, anyway?"

It was a question he never asked runaways; they rarely told the truth about things like names and addresses. But against his better judgment, he was damn curious about just who she was and what she was hiding. Maybe if he asked her outright, she'd slip up and tell him something.

He could see the hesitation on her face, so he gave her the same line he always gave new arrivals. "If you're going to be staying with us, we'll have to call you something."

She seemed confused for a moment or two, as if making up her mind about what to tell him.

"M-my name?"

"Yeah. You do have a name, don't you?"

"Well, yes..." She broke off, and then smiled at him, a knockout of a smile that lit up her whole angelic face. "Of course—my name," she said with more conviction. And she offered him her small, slender hand.

Shifting the kid and the bag around to be able to take it, he instinctively steeled himself against reacting to the feel of her skin next to his. But it had been inevitable since the first moment he saw her, standing there in the train station, looking lost and alone. And he knew it.

As he wrapped his bigger, rougher hand around hers, he felt it, that tingle of recognition, a kind of spark passing from her hand to his. The kind of sensation that told him he was going to want her and want her bad before this was all over. Damn it, anyway.

He dropped her hand. "So your name, what is it?" he growled, doing his damnedest to stay cool.

"Angel." With more than a touch of mischief, she announced, "You can call me Angel."

"Yeah, right."

Angel, indeed. Who did she think she was kidding? But he found himself smiling as he led the way to the truck.

THE MINUTE SHE CLIMBED gingerly into Finn Sheridan's pickup truck, she knew she was in trouble. It was too small, too intimate in there, just her and the man and the boy.

Derek snuggled up against her from the middle of the seat, winding his tiny fingers around a long tendril of her ghastly hair, whispering "Angel" as he pulled on it. She winced, but didn't have the heart to disengage him.

Meanwhile, Mr. Tough Guy levered himself behind the wheel and pulled his door shut with a resounding slam. It was a very final sound. Angie's heart sank, and she wondered, not for the first time, what in the world she thought she was doing, seeking shelter with a complete stranger.

But neither beggars nor runaways could be choosers. So she tried to settle in as comfortably as she could in the cold, damp truck, shivering and waiting for the heat to kick on. Even though she was much too close to Finn Sheridan to be anything as mundane as comfortable. He sat over there, one wrist dangling over the top of the steering wheel as he stared out the front window, paying no attention to her, driving them farther and farther into the night.

She was close enough to see the small white scar slicing his eyebrow, the dark hair drifting over his collar and the stark elegance of his profile. She pulled her eyes away, but it didn't stop her nose from sending signals to her brain about the tantalizing scent of an outdoorsy man in a weathered leather jacket.

Oh, yes, she knew he was over there, silent and forbidding. Even with her eyes closed, she knew.

Meanwhile, Derek nodded off, leaning well into her lap, mumbling soft words about angels, and Finn Sheridan drove on. And on.

"Where are we going?" she asked finally, as the last lights of civilization dimmed behind them.

"Shh," he returned irritably. "Do you want to wake the kid?"

"You should've thought of that before you dragged him out so late at night. It's not my fault he's still up."

"He's not. He's asleep. And he'll stay that way if you keep your voice down."

"How dare you..." she began, before she remembered it was his truck and his young charge and she was entirely at his mercy. In a calmer, softer tone, she asked politely, "Where exactly are we headed?"

"Out of town."

Well, that didn't tell her a whole heck of a lot, did it? "I can see that," she said testily. "Where, specifically, out of town?"

"'Where, specifically'?" he echoed. "You know, you talk kind of prissy. You just don't sound like the kind of woman who'd be caught dead in that coat. Or with that hair."

"I happen to like my hair just fine," she snapped back. "And as for the coat, well, I'm certainly glad I have it, because it's freezing in your stupid truck."

"That's what winter is like hereabouts, Angel. Get used to it."

"I don't intend to stick around that long."

He cast a sardonic glance over her way. "I guess you're from a warmer clime, huh? No Southern accent, though. Arizona? California?"

So much for subtlety. The man was digging, and they both knew it. Not that she had any intention of satisfying his curiosity. "Never mind where I'm from. At the moment, I'm more interested in where I'm going."

She peered out at the thin ribbon of desolate road, unlighted and unpaved. On every side she saw flat, still, snow-wrapped darkness, broken only by an occasional light from a farmhouse. Lovely. She despised farms with every fiber of her career-girl body. And she was beginning to have a very bad feeling about Finn Sheridan and his shelter.

"Heavenly Acres," he said finally. "We'll be there in a minute or two."

"Heavenly Acres? What kind of name is that?"

But Mr. Tough Guy offered no excuses for the sissy name of his place. All he said was, "I didn't name it."

And then he cranked the wheel, angling the truck onto a winding gravel road and finally pulling it to a stop between a small white farmhouse and a big old red barn.

Another person might have found the small farm charming, bathed in gentle moonlight, sparkled with frost. Angie felt ill.

Clearly paying no attention to her distress, Finn Sheridan gently tugged Derek out his side of the truck, leaving Angie to open her door and clamber down all by herself. As her boot hit the ground, crunching on hard, cold snow, she was assailed by a rush of frigid air and a very familiar smell wafting over from the barn.

That smell removed any lingering doubts as to what exactly she'd gotten herself into. Manure. Deep manure.

Sagging against the side of Finn Sheridan's rusty pickup, Angie allowed herself a good long moment of self-pity. "Was it so much to ask?" she whispered. "All I ever wanted was to get out of Nebraska, and to never, ever see another tractor or another cow. It wasn't so much, was it?"

But here she was, back where she started, with the smell of manure hanging heavy in the air, with all of her precious dreams for a life in the big city smashed to smithereens. It was enough to make a strong woman cry.

"Are you coming?"

Stiffening her spine, Angie turned to face him. "Yes, I'm coming," she said coolly. Any idea of crying at this nasty turn of fate would have to be squelched. She was too frustrated and too exhausted to waste energy on tears. Besides, she was stuck here in this wasteland. Might as well get a good night's sleep and worry about her problems tomorrow.

"One night," she told herself bravely. "I can stand it for one night."

Hoisting Derek over his shoulder, Finn held out a hand to help her up the porch steps. "Sorry to disappoint you, Angel, but I think you'll be staying more than one night."

"No—" she began, but he cut her off.

"I'm not planning another trip into town for at least a few days, so you'll have to wait." He smiled grimly. "Unless you'd like to walk."

"But why didn't you tell me that before you got me out here?" She felt like stamping her foot and throwing a tantrum. With the day she'd had, any number of behavioral aberrations was possible.

Finn Sheridan only shrugged, which made her even madder.

"How could you?" she cried.

"Keep your voice down, will you? Sound carries around here."

He shifted the burden in his arms, nestling Derek's small head against his broad chest. It was a lovely image, but it made Angie want to find the nearest rock and bash his strong, silent head in. How dare he stand there, looking like every woman's fantasy man, at the same time keeping her prisoner on a *farm?*

"How could you?" she asked again, in a lower, more seething sort of voice. "How dare you bring me all the way out into the middle of nowhere without at least doing me the courtesy of warning me that you wouldn't take me back?"

The insufferable Finn Sheridan merely gazed at her with an unpleasant look on his face. "I will take you back in a few days. I didn't think it would matter. Runaways aren't usually that picky about a day or two here or there."

"I'm no runaw—" she started to shout, but he'd already retrieved her bag from the truck and swept inside the house, leaving her alone on the freezing porch. Besides, he was right. She *was* a runaway, and she had nowhere better to go, not today or tomorrow or the next day. And they both knew it.

A sign hanging over the porch flapped in the stiff winter wind, and Angie wheeled, startled at the sudden noise. *Heavenly Acres Farm,* it read, with the words curving over a dark portrait of a winged, haloed angel, whose ditsy blond hair flowed past her wings and down to the hem of her gauzy white gown. No wonder Derek thought she was an angel.

"Heavenly Acres, my foot," she muttered, pushing open the front door. "More like hell, if you ask me."

She didn't know what she'd expected from a retreat for runaways, but nothing like this. This was a cozy, cutesy little farmhouse, complete with overstuffed chairs and lace doilies. Except for Derek sleeping sweetly on the sofa, this was her mother's fussy front parlor to a T.

She lifted her eyes to Finn Sheridan's dark, uncommunicative face. "You can't be serious."

"I gather you're not crazy about the accommodations."

"Well, I'm surprised, if that's what you mean."

"Naah." His gaze swept up and down her, resting somewhere near the fuzzy lapel of her coat. "I get the idea you don't think much of rural life."

"Well, no, I... I mean, I—"

"City girl, huh?"

If she explained the particulars of her feeling for farms—that she'd grown up on one, hated every minute of it, taken off to Washington, D.C. to make her fortune, and now suddenly been forced to leave it all behind—he'd find out who she was and send her packing before the hour was out. *Lie, Angie,* she told herself. *It's your new way of life.*

"Yeah, that's right," she whispered. "City girl. Never been on a farm before in my life."

"Not what you expected?"

"Well, I haven't seen much of it yet, have I? But I guess I thought a homeless shelter would look different from this." Angie glanced around at her surroundings, suddenly feeling very suspicious. "Hey, wait a minute. Where are all the kids? I thought you kept a whole bunch of homeless children here."

"Not in the house. I live in the house." His face gave nothing away as he hitched a thumb over his shoulder. "They're in the bunkhouses out back—one for boys and one for girls."

"Oh, out back." She nodded, accepting his word for the time being, damping down her newly skeptical

nature. Everything certainly looked aboveboard and
well cared for around here. Certainly no hint of any
nefarious activity. . . .

"Yeah," he continued. "Everybody should be in
bed by now. I'll be taking Derek out as soon as you're
settled." As an afterthought he added, "Although the
other guys are going to be disappointed I didn't bring
a new kid back. They like to hassle newcomers."

"I don't qualify as a newcomer?"

"Count your blessings," he said gruffly. "Anyway, I can't see sticking you in with the girls. They'd
hate it—think I was sending in a spy. So you'll be
staying up here."

"In the house, you mean?"

Without wasting any time, he leaned over to pick up
her duffel bag, and then tossed it halfway up the stairs
with one easy motion. "Yeah. With me."

As he bent, his jeans cupped the tight, hard curve of
his bottom, and Angie found it suddenly difficult to
breathe.

"Excuse me?" she managed, trying desperately to
clear her head. Just the two of them, all alone in the
house? Was that what he'd just said? Or was it just the
tantalizing picture of his backside that was making her
imagine things? "Did you say I'd be . . . with you?"

That got a dark look out of Mr. Tough Guy. "Don't
sweat it. You'll stay in my room. I'll take the couch
down here."

"But I—"

"Look, I haven't got time to fool with this," he said
impatiently. "Top of the stairs, on the left. If you end
up staying longer than a couple of days, we'll make

other arrangements, but for right now, this is the way it is."

"It isn't like you're giving me a choice," she muttered, but she scampered up the first few steps, anxious to be away from him. Behind her, she could hear Derek mumbling sleepily as Finn prepared to haul the boy off to bed.

"Oh, and by the way..." Finn called after her.

Her hand stilled on the banister, but she stayed where she was. "Yes?"

"Extra toothbrushes in the medicine cabinet. And since I don't suppose you brought anything to sleep in, you can borrow what you want from my drawers. Paw around—I don't care."

He might not have cared, but she did, as she decided *not* to paw, but to very carefully remove one of his T-shirts from the top drawer. She couldn't believe she'd been stupid enough to forget to buy a nightgown when she'd done her tour of the department store. It was even more infuriating that Finn Sheridan had known just by looking at her that she'd need to borrow something. It was insulting. She felt unprepared and irresponsible. And it was all his fault.

Nonetheless, she had nothing else to wear to bed, so she had to take the T-shirt. But she wasn't touching anything extra of his unless she absolutely had to, and she pushed his drawer shut with a satisfying slam. No surprise, it was freezing in the drafty farmhouse, and she hesitated a moment before stripping down to her underwear and quickly donning the T-shirt.

She told herself she was too tired to notice that it smelled like him. "You don't know what he smelled like," she chastised herself loudly. "You were no-where near the man."

Ha. She'd sat not two feet from him in the front seat of the pickup, where she couldn't miss the dangerous scent of Finn Sheridan. He'd smelled like outdoors, like crisp winter breezes and old, worn leather, like a man who worked himself hard and cleaned up beau-tifully.

And now, here in his room, she could still catch the faint, alluring odor she'd already identified as his. From the shirts hanging in the closet to the clean clothes in his drawers, it all smelled like Finn. She couldn't stand it.

"Maybe I'll get a cold in this icebox," she said sav-agely. "You can't smell with a cold."

It took a good deal of courage to get herself to crawl into *his* bed. But it was so darned cold standing there in nothing but an oversize T-shirt—that she finally had no choice. Closing her eyes, she peeled back the cov-ers with one rapid yank, vaulting inside, telling her-self his bed was as good as any, quickly casting out any rogue images of him sprawled across it or wound up in it.

It was a soft, old-fashioned, welcoming bed, the kind whose springs jangled and wheezed if she moved too quickly. It felt wonderful to be lying down after so many miles and so many traumas, to have any kind of refuge from the disaster her life had become.

But it was still Finn Sheridan's bed. And she wasn't really safe at all, was she? Not with him prowling around, casting smoky glances with those beautiful blue eyes, stuffing his hands into the pockets of his already too-tight jeans. . . .

"Forget that," she said out loud, forcefully banishing his image from her mind. If she couldn't forget him completely, the least she could do was pretend to think about something else. "I have plenty of other things to think about. Like the fact that I'm still an icicle." A pretty quilt and a couple of blankets now covered her, so she knew she would warm up fairly quickly, but it didn't help her frosty mood at the moment.

"Go to sleep," she commanded herself. "Stop thinking about that man and his bed and his T-shirt."

But the minute she closed her eyes, she had visions of herself as Goldilocks, snuggling her golden ringlets into somebody else's sheets. And a very large, very angry man—who bore a striking resemblance to Finn Sheridan—came crashing into her room, showing off a whole mouthful of sharp, pointy teeth, roaring, "Who's been sleeping in my bed?"

"Papa Bear doesn't have teeth like that," she murmured drowsily.

But the raging man in her dream just roared louder, beating his fists against his smooth, broad chest. "Mmm. Nice," she whispered. "Very nice."

And then he bent down over her, deep into the bed, baring his teeth and aiming for her neck. "Oh, yes," she murmured into her pillow, shifting restlessly in the throes of her fantasy world.

"Oh, yes," she said again, arching her back, offering up her neck to his erotic bite. He leaned closer, and her pulse raced as she almost felt the pressure of his teeth....

Clomp, clomp, clomp.

That didn't sound like the man in her dream. She ignored the clumsy intrusion, choosing to stay in the fantasy world she'd concocted for herself.

But there it was again, louder this time. *Clomp, clomp.*

Against her will, the sounds penetrated her sleepy mind, interfering with the erotic images in her brain. Who was that, tromping across the hardwood floors, puncturing her fantasies?

"Go 'way," she mumbled, trying to pull the pieces of her wicked lover back together again.

But it was too late. *Clomp, clomp, clomp,* she heard again—as if somebody big and fierce and *real* was in the house and stalking her.

Angie stiffened in the strange bed, dragging herself awake enough to open one eye and crack it toward the shadowy door. Still securely closed. Nothing there.

"Just old house noises," she told herself sleepily, snuggling back into her pillow. "Water pipes or something."

All was silent for a long pause. And then it started.

"Hooo..." came howling through the window, fading and then intensifying, like some horrible set of moans and groans from a haunted house. "Hooo..."

She sat bolt upright in bed, clutching the quilt. "Who's there?" she shouted.

But the only answer was that horrifying howl and the rattle of glass in the windowframe.

"It's just the wind, and it doesn't scare me," she said shakily. She eased out of the bed, taking three cautious steps in the direction of the window. "Better make sure it's latched," she whispered, inching closer.

Until she saw it. A greenish, ghoulish face, floating in the darkness outside her window.

Angie screamed and screamed and screamed some more, frozen to the floor, afraid to move or run or do anything but stand there and wail like a banshee. Vaguely, she heard footsteps pounding behind her as the door was wrenched open and a large body hurtled inside.

"What is it? Are you all right?" he asked, but she couldn't stop screaming.

There was a strong, solid, very real man right next to her, offering a lifeline, and she did the only thing that made a particle of sense. She threw her arms around that warm, naked chest and held on for dear life.

Chapter Four

"Angel," he murmured, and she held on tighter.

His heart beat rapidly under her ear, and she forgot all about green ghouls and horrible screams. This was sanctuary...this was heaven.

His skin pulsed hot against her cheek, and she was so very cold. All that lay between her and his chest was the thin fabric of her T-shirt, not nearly enough of a barrier. She was acutely aware of her shirt and her thin panties, so little, all in all. She could've been wearing a down coat and it still would've seemed inadequate matched up to his inviting bare chest and his jean-clad legs. She could feel him, smell him, breathe him, and she wanted to be closer still.

Some small part of her knew it was incredibly dangerous to press up against him like this, to close her eyes and slide her fingers over his hard, smooth muscles, but he felt wonderful. She couldn't remember the last time she'd been held so tightly, or felt so safe and warm.

"Finn," she breathed, wrapping herself around him. Maybe it was that she was tired, or scared, or lonely. Whatever the reason, she couldn't resist, couldn't pull away. She told herself she knew exactly where she was and what she was doing.

And then his fingers crept under the tail of her shirt, burning her, brushing the lace on her panties where they curved high on her hip. Suddenly she was on fire, blazing out from the small spot of skin where his fingers touched. This was like dancing on the edge of a cliff.

She caught her breath, trying not to move and break the spell. But a soft moan escaped her. She heard him mutter something under his breath as he took her chin in one hand and gazed deep into her eyes.

"Why?" he murmured.

His lips were so close, and she trembled. She lifted her mouth to him, wondering if he would kiss her, afraid he would, desperate he wouldn't.

He didn't.

He backed off unsteadily, leaving her feeling alone and bereft on her side of the bedroom. "What's this all about, Angel?" he asked darkly.

"About?" she echoed, confused.

"You screamed," he reminded her.

"Oh, right. I screamed."

"I thought I was rescuing a damsel in distress." He rammed his hands into the pockets of his pants. Soft and worn, the jeans rode low on his hips, and she knew without question that he wasn't wearing a damn thing underneath them. "I didn't realize there would be an ambush."

"An ambush?" Oh Lord, he meant her. And he was right. What in the world had she thought she was doing, clinging to him like some tropical vine? "It was the window," she mumbled, feeling her face flame with embarrassment.

He arched an eyebrow. "The window?"

"Yes, the window." She stiffened her spine and raised her chin. "There was someone—or something—out there. I saw it. It was green, and it was howling."

"A green, howling monster?" he asked dubiously. "Are you sure you weren't dreaming?"

"No, I wasn't dreaming." Only now did she realize that by straightening her posture, she was practically thrusting her breasts in his direction. Holy smokes. She snatched a pillow off the bed and clamped it to her front. It didn't cover all that much more of her, but it made her feel safer, somehow. As if his moody blue eyes could penetrate mere cotton, but not feathers and down.

Trying not to feel ridiculous hanging on to a pillow for dear life, she stated firmly, "There was something hideous at my window, and it was definitely howling at me."

"Well, there's nothing there now," he said after a pause.

But his gaze was nowhere near the window. Instead, his eyes were directed at her, as if he were drinking in the sight of her, all flushed and bothered and half naked. If she didn't know better, she'd have thought he was as turned on by the dark intimacy of their situation as she was.

"Maybe you should actually look out the window before you conclude there's nothing there," she said sharply, hugging her pillow closer.

Frowning, he swept past her, and then stood at the window with his smooth, naked back turned toward her, as he stared out into the darkness. His shoulders were broad and strong, and she couldn't quite believe she'd fingered them with such familiarity only moments ago. Her hands twitched at the idea of touching him again. She grabbed a fistful of pillow to remind her to keep her hands to herself.

"Well, I guess you win," he said reluctantly. "Looks like there might be something stuck in the tree—like a kite or something. I'll, uh, go out and check. See what's up. Maybe you should just go back to bed. I'm sure everything's okay now."

Okay? How could anything be okay when she was standing there drooling at him, willing her body and her mind to stop playing these awful games?

"Right," she returned, although she couldn't for the life of her remember what he'd said in the first place.

"It won't take long to check it out." He edged back around her and made for the door. "Go to bed, okay?"

His hand fell to the knob, and she said quickly, "I'd feel better if you could come back and tell me what you found."

"Yeah, okay. Just go to sleep, all right?"

"To sleep. Right." She sank to the edge of the bed, still clutching the pillow. But as he took a step out into the hall, she began to think better of seeing him one more time on this crazy night. "You know, Finn," she said suddenly. "You don't have to...I mean, I'm sure I'll be fine, so you don't have to come back up here if you don't want to."

He cast her an odd glance. "I said I'll be back."

"Okay. If you're sure."

"I'm sure."

"Oh, and Finn...?"

After a moment, his eyes flickered up to hers. "Yeah?"

"Thank you."

He shrugged. "It's no big deal."

"And I'm, well, sorry, you know, that I kind of leaped on you when you came in."

A hint of a smile played around his narrow lips. "Leaped? You mean when you threw yourself at me like a bat out of hell?"

Warmth suffused her cheeks. "Yeah, that."

"It's okay. You were scared." He lifted his perfect shoulders in an eloquent shrug. "I understand."

As he slipped out the door, Angie remembered the hard, hot feel of those shoulders under her fingers and under her cheek. She remembered sidling herself up against him like a hungry kitten.

"I'm glad he understands," she whispered. "Because I sure don't."

As she retreated to the relative safety of Finn Sheridan's bed, she could hear the sound of his footsteps, padding down the stairs and into the main part of the house. And then nothing.

A pipe whistled softly, a few floorboards groaned, but that was it. Angie just sat there, bolt upright in his bed, clutching the quilt up under her chin like an old maid in a bawdy house.

After what seemed an eternity, she heard the muffled sound of his footsteps climb the steps, and then stop outside her room. There was silence for a long, awkward pause, as she imagined him standing there in the hallway, deciding what to do. She wondered if he'd put on a shirt yet.

"He would've had to put on a shirt," she muttered. "He went outside, for pity's sake. In the cold." But the memory of his smooth, strong, *bare* torso and how it had felt against her refused to go away.

Finally, he tapped gently, twice, on her door. "Angel?" he asked softly. "You awake?"

She cleared her throat. "Yes," she managed. "I'm awake."

There were a few soft clicks from the direction of the door handle, as if, on the other side, Finn was resting his hand on it, making up his mind whether or not to come in.

"There was nothing to worry about," he said finally.

Angie tried to relax. At least he was staying safely on his side of the door. "Nothing to worry about?" she echoed.

"Just a couple of the kids, pulling a prank. They painted a green face on a piece of sheet and then ran it up outside your window on a broom. Nothing really, but scary, I guess, if you don't understand a certain dopey sense of humor."

Nothing really? She'd been scared half out of her wits! She'd been pushed into screaming and yelling and getting way too intimate with Finn Sheridan. She felt like an idiot. And it was those kids' fault.

"Kids," she grumbled. "A bunch of real charmers."

"They have their moments." She could feel his smile through the door, with that tight, superior twitch to his lips. "If it's any consolation," he went on, "they pull something equally dumb every time we have a new arrival. It's their way of making new people feel welcome."

"All in all, I'd have felt more welcome with a good night's sleep."

"Sorry. I thought you'd be safe—not being the usual kind of new kid."

"Oh, that's okay," she said finally, although it really wasn't.

But even if it was an annoying trick, it wasn't Finn's fault. His tough-guy attitude might be less than agreeable, but hadn't he picked her up, given her a place to sleep and come running when she screamed? No, it wasn't his fault.

"Thank you," she murmured. "I'm sorry for all the trouble."

"No trouble."

"Okay, well, thanks again."

There was a pause. "Good night, Angel," he said softly.

"Good night, Finn."

And then the footsteps retreated once more, and she knew she was alone. She didn't know what to make of any of it—from her crazy dream to the hideous green face to the sanctuary of Finn's embrace.

"Making me feel welcome," she whispered in the dark.

Wasn't that exactly the problem? Shivering, she rubbed her hands against her upper arms. She had felt entirely too welcome inside the hard circle of Finn Sheridan's arms.

IT WAS MORNING, ungodly early, but daylight, nonetheless. Still feeling bleary and confused, Angie recognized the smells and sounds of breakfast—bacon and eggs, rattling pans, the rumble of voices down in the kitchen.

Bacon and eggs? Voices? She lived alone!

She sat up. "Where am I?" she mumbled. As she looked around, all she saw were rumpled bedclothes and several pieces of old-fashioned furniture. "This isn't my apartment."

As she tried to clear her head, the events of the past few days returned in a jumble. Angie slid back under the covers, groaning. It all came back now. She might be blocking out a few of the sordid details, but she did remember Finn Sheridan clearly. Very clearly.

She shook her head, trying not to dwell on her own shortcomings. After all, no one could be expected to handle images of Finn and his bare skin on an empty stomach. "Better think about him later," she ordered herself.

Her stomach growled loudly, reminding her there were other things besides Finn to consider. Although she hadn't eaten bacon and eggs for breakfast since she'd left her parents' farm—usually drinking six cups of coffee—she had to admit it smelled pretty darned good, wafting up through the floorboards. And against all odds after the crazy night she'd had, she was hungry.

Too bad Finn was probably lurking downstairs, lording over the food. She had no desire to clash with him again. Well, maybe she had a bit of desire, but her head knew better.

Another outrageous rumble from her stomach made up her mind for her. Quickly, she dashed into her clothes and splashed some water on her face, rushing to get down to the kitchen and into the food. And coffee. She needed caffeine.

"Finn or no Finn," she told herself sternly, "once you have coffee, you will feel like a human being again."

The closer she got to the kitchen, the louder the clatter of voices became. She heard no trace of Finn's low, distinctive drawl, just the high pitch of childish exuberance.

"Oh, dear," she lamented. "I forgot about the kids."

Taking a deep breath, she hesitated outside the door, trying to fortify herself for this little encounter with what sounded like twenty or thirty rambunctious tots.

With six younger brothers, Angie had no illusions about the dubious charm of drippy noses and scraped knees, of grubby little fingers and bratty little insults. With so many brothers, she'd had frogs in her oatmeal and worms in her bed, fistfights on the playground and spit-wads across the dinner table. Angie

Marie Boone was not terribly tolerant of small children.

As she pushed open the door and took a look around, she realized that there were only five or six of them—even if they were making enough noise for three times that many—and they ranged in age from about ten to at least fourteen. Derek, the sweet little boy from last night, was absent. This bunch was an older and angrier variety of child, staring openly, looking hostile and surly and tough as nails.

Angie stared right back. She reminded herself that these were the same little sweethearts who'd paraded a "ghost" outside her window in the wee hours of the night. Intimidation was the only tactic she could think of at the moment.

"So you're Angel." The biggest one pushed his way to the forefront of the group. He was kind of cute, with dark hair and sleepy eyes, but his black leather gloves, complete with cutout fingers, sort of wrecked the image. As Angie watched, he flexed his hands inside the wretched gloves, clearly putting on his best tough act. "Finn told us to watch for you. I'm Zero."

"Zero?" She tried not to smile. But at this time of the morning, without benefit of coffee, she couldn't be held responsible for a few wayward grins.

"Somethin' wrong with that?"

"Uh, no," she said quickly. "Zero is a lovely name."

"Yeah, well, I like it." He pooched out his lip and just stood there, glaring, until she was forced to speak.

"Where is Finn this morning?"

"Why?" Zero's dark eyes were taunting. "Can't deal with us kids all by yourself, huh, lady?"

"Just being polite."

"Yeah, well, we don't go in much for politeness around here."

"I can tell." She edged a bit farther into the room, ignoring whatever was left of Zero's macho posturing. "Is there any coffee?" she asked hopefully.

"Don't you know caffeine is bad for you?" Zero demanded. "We don't keep stuff that's bad for you around here."

Angie was finding this all very hard to take. Since when was caffeine a major crime? "Is this a joke?"

"No, it's not a joke!" Zero glowered at her. "It's in the rules—number two—big as life. I woulda already told you, but you keep jawin' at me. I was supposed to lay down the law as soon as you woke up—that's the way we do it."

"The rules?" she echoed doubtfully. Surely whatever disciplinary regulations Finn used to keep a bunch of children in line didn't apply to her. "I don't think—"

"Number one," he said loudly, holding up a finger. As his voice rose, a small brown tabby cat shot out from under the kitchen table and streaked past Angie.

"Now look what you've done," she chided. "You scared the cat."

He ignored her and the cat, as he launched his list of rules. "Number one—everybody pulls their weight to keep the farm running. Number two—no drugs, no cigarettes, no booze . . ." He smiled snidely. "And no caffeine. Three—nobody is forced to call home or tell their parents where they are, but they can if they want to."

Right. Like calling her parents was high on her priority list at the age of twenty-eight. But she'd give the kid credit; he was very good at sounding like the voice of doom. Meanwhile, on he went with his little litany, and Angie tried to pretend she was properly impressed.

Zero was up to four fingers. "Nobody has to say anything about where they came from or why they left unless they want to."

That last one was fine by her. For the first time, she began to understand that landing at Heavenly Acres Farm might not be such a bad deal, after all. If she got food and shelter and didn't have to tell what she was running away from, maybe she was really in the right place.

"Five," Zero went on grimly. "Anybody who screws up any of the rules is out. Six—anybody who endangers himself or anyone else is out."

Thoughts of the FBI and the mob flickered briefly in Angie's brain. If either group found out where she was, danger was a real possibility. But how could they find her? *She* didn't even know where she was.

"I don't think your rules apply to me," she tried.

"You're here, so they apply. That's the way it is, lady."

It was too early in the morning to disagree with him, especially with no prospects of coffee. Stifling a yawn, she slid into a chair at the table, eying a nearby platter of bacon. "Okay, okay. If you say so."

"Right." Zero's little-boy smile took on a nasty twinge. "So what do you want—chickens or pigs?"

"Excuse me?"

"Chickens or pigs?"

"I'm afraid I don't understand."

"You forget already, Angel? Rule number one— everybody pulls their weight. And right now you get to choose—go get eggs out from under the chickens, or slop the pigs." The boy shrugged, but there was mischief in his eyes. "You're lucky—we don't usually give new kids a choice."

Ignoring the siren call of the bacon, Angie pushed herself back from the table. "I hardly qualify as a new kid."

"Too bad. You wanna eat, you gotta contribute. And chickens and pigs is what's left."

"I don't care what's left." She was working hard not to bite Mr. Zero's head off. He might think he was a tough guy, but he'd never seen the dark side of a midlevel government grunt on a bad day. "I'm twice your age, mister," she said with a definite chill. "As a result, I don't take orders from you. Got it?"

"Yeah, well, you don't got a choice." Zero advanced on her, making little slits of his sleepy brown eyes. "Chickens or pigs?"

"You can take your chickens and your pigs—"

"That's enough." Finn's voice came sharp and hard, cutting them both off as he edged in the back door.

Immediately, she felt the electricity of his presence, zinging across the crowded kitchen and stopping her cold. She remembered what it was like to have his hand on her thigh, and to feel his arms hard around her. But that was in the dark of night, and this was the cool gray morning.

At least he was wearing a shirt this time—a plain black T-shirt, under a battered leather jacket. Covering up his beautiful chest was a crime. And a blessing.

"Both of you, back off," he commanded.

Looking very sulky, Zero stuffed his hands in his pockets, but he did manage to meander back a step or two. "Finn, she has to obey the rules. She has to, right?"

Softly, Finn announced, "Absolutely. No exceptions."

"Now wait just a second—" Angie started.

"No," he returned, and his voice and his eyes were cold. "You wait just a second. You're the guest here, I'm in charge. Did you forget that? Or did you think you were going to waltz in here and act like you owned the place?"

"Why on earth would I want to own *this* place?" She'd been duly annoyed with Zero's uppity act, but she could deal with that. Now being chastised in front of a room full of kids, she really began to seethe. "But, as you might imagine, I do not appreciate being taken to task by a child."

"Zero has been here longer than anyone besides me. That earns him the right to dole out chores." Finn's jaw clenched. "If you can't take on a simple chore, then you don't belong here."

"But I wasn't planning on staying," she reminded him.

"You've already stayed," he reminded her right back. "Unless you're thinking of walking back to town right now, I suggest you play by our rules."

Angie held on to her temper by pretending that Finn Sheridan had a bullet hole right between his beautiful blue eyes. "Couldn't you reconsider, given the fact that I, unlike your other guests, am over the age of fourteen?"

"No."

The man was not only irritating beyond belief, but was stubborn, too. "Why not?" she persevered.

"Because you've already had too much special treatment."

Through the red haze impairing her vision, she could see that the children in the room were hanging on every word of this rather heated discussion. And she began to get an inkling of why Finn Sheridan was taking the hard line. Understandably enough, he didn't want to lose face in front of his charges.

"Could I speak with you privately?" she asked coolly.

He considered. "Okay," he said finally. "Three minutes."

Without bothering to see if she'd follow, Finn swept from the room. Behind them, the cacophony of voices rose immediately. *Terrific,* she groused. She hadn't been here twenty-four hours, and she was already causing a scandal.

Trailing behind Finn, Angie found herself in a small room off the living room at the front of the house. Since it was packed with filing cabinets, a scruffy desk and bits and pieces of computer equipment, she deduced it was Finn's office.

After tossing his leather jacket over the side of the desk, he pulled a creaky wooden chair around backward so he could straddle it. With his arms propped on the back of the chair, he glanced down at his watch, held up a finger while he waited for the big hand to hit the twelve, and then said, "Go."

"Go?"

He smiled up at her. It was a calm, infuriating, arrogant smile. "Give it your best shot."

By that, she assumed he meant that she was free to try to get herself excused from odious farm chores. She was prepared to launch her best effort, but she really didn't appreciate his attitude. "I'm not a child, and I'm certainly not a delinquent. Perhaps you should save the stern parental treatment for someone who is impressed by it."

There was a pause, as Finn's cold blue eyes raked her. "Why do I want so damn badly to turn you over my knee?"

A tiny, very dangerous part of her thought she might like that a lot. Crossing her arms over her chest, Angie said primly, "I suppose that's the way you frighten all these children into behaving. Threatening corporal punishment, I mean."

"Nobody till you."

"Well, it's not working. I'm not afraid of you."

"Maybe you should be." He stood up suddenly, and she took an involuntary step backward. "Maybe you should be scared of me, Angel."

She tried to remember to keep breathing. *You're not afraid of him,* she told herself bravely. So why was she trembling?

"There's no reason to bully me."

"Here, sit down," he ordered her, pulling a folding chair up next to the desk. Reluctantly, he retreated to his chair, and she scooted into hers before he changed his mind and threatened spanking again.

"Well?" He cocked an eyebrow. "Your time's almost up, Angel. Are you going to try to bargain with me or not?"

Bargain? Not on his life. "Reason," she said slowly. "I was going to try to reason with you."

"So get to it."

"Well, I mean, it's just that..." She set her jaw firmly and sat up straight. "I simply fail to understand why your, shall we say, childish rules should apply to me."

"My rules keep this place running, Angel. If I make exceptions, it stops working. For everybody—especially me."

"But I don't want to fool with chickens and pigs. It's sort of nonsensical, don't you think? I mean, just to make a point."

"And what happens if I let you off the hook? Why should Zero or any of the others do what they're supposed to if you don't?"

"But it's outrageous!"

"It works. That's my bottom line."

"How can it be working? Those kids are clearly out of control!" Angie leaned closer and tried to show him the error of his ways. "Your rules are okay, I guess, but they don't really cover much, do they? I mean, mostly they just tell the kids to do a few chores and cut out caffeine, and then they can do whatever they want."

"That's about the size of it."

"But juvenile delinquents shouldn't have that much freedom, or that much authority. I mean, my goodness, ordering grown-ups around?"

Finn shrugged. "So Zero has a chance to feel in control. Why not?"

"Why not?" she scoffed. "Because he's going to run wild, like last night, with that thing at my window. And today—listen to the noise from the kitchen, and from outside, too, for that matter. Not to mention the fact that he frightened the poor little kitten who was in the kitchen, and he didn't even care. I happen to like cats!" she finished up angrily.

"Good. I like cats, too. And I've never seen Zero mistreat any of the animals."

"Well, those kids should be in school," Angie persevered, "learning some discipline, learning how to get along in the world."

"School failed them," he said flatly. "Hell, the world failed them. I won't fail them."

"So you let them walk all over you?"

"A little freedom—a little responsibility—is hardly walking all over anybody."

"Talk about the inmates running the asylum!"

"Look, lady, you don't know anything about this place or these kids." He rose from behind the desk, and the expression on his face was positively stony. "I don't care if you don't like the way I do things. I know what works. You don't. End of discussion."

"But—"

"End of discussion," he repeated. "Did you decide yet whether you want chickens or pigs?"

"You're enjoying this," she accused.

A hint of a smile played around the corners of his narrow lips. "It's not every day I get somebody my own age to play with."

"This isn't playing." Practically smoking with suppressed anger, Angie rose to her feet and made for the door. Over her shoulder, she shot back, "This is war."

And then she stalked back through the kitchen, yanked a basket off a hook on the wall, shouted "Chickens" at Zero before he had a chance to ask that same stupid question one more time, and slammed out the back door.

"I'll show them chickens," she muttered between clenched teeth.

But she calmed down quickly. By the time she spotted the hen house and walked through the frigid air to get there, she had cooled off considerably. She remembered years of egg collecting as a child, and she knew the worst thing she could do was take out her temper on the hens.

Calmly, quietly, she clucked and murmured sweet nothings to the chickens, filling her basket in no time. She knew Zero and his pals had expected her to come back pecked to distraction and covered with eggshells and bits of yolk, so it was with triumph that she marched in the back door with nary a scratch and not one broken egg. Finn and Zero were both there, waiting for her, looking smug and self-satisfied.

All the better, she thought. *Think you're throwing me a curve? We'll just see who strikes out, tough guy.*

Smiling sweetly, she held out the basket. "Eggs, anyone?"

"That didn't take long," Finn noted dryly. His eyes narrowed as he glanced down at the eggs and then back up at her. He didn't say anything, but she caught the speculative look in his blue eyes, and she wondered suddenly if her little triumph was worth the risk.

She'd just given away an important clue about herself, and where she'd spent the early years of her life. She might as well have tied a sign that said Farm Girl around her neck. And of all the people in the world, Finn Sheridan was definitely sharp enough to pick up on it.

Angie set the eggs down quickly and turned away from his penetrating gaze. She was going to have to be smarter if she planned to stick around and not get caught. She took a deep breath. A whole lot smarter.

There was only one tactic she could think of to make this work, and it wasn't going to be easy. Nonetheless, she told herself sternly, *Keep your mouth shut and stay out of his way.*

The new motto of Angie Marie Boone, sex kitten on the run.

Chapter Five

"Hello there, Ms. Cow. What's your name?" she asked in a cheerful, if shaky voice.

She really didn't like cows. Their heads were too big, for one thing. And she'd been whipped mercilessly by their tails more times than she cared to recall when she'd tried milking back on her parents' farm. Back then, she'd bribed her brother, Darryl, to do the milking for her.

This time there was no Darryl to beg. So she didn't have a choice, did she?

After all, she was keeping her cool and staying out of trouble. When assigned to milk the cow, she figured she'd better get it over with and damp down her irrational distaste for the bovine set rather than risk getting into a fight with Finn.

"Nice cow," she said encouragingly, coming up to the lumpy thing from the front. She felt more than a little ridiculous as she patted it on the head. "I know you don't know me, but we're going to get along just fine, aren't we?"

It just chewed its cud, giving her the once-over with its big, sad brown eyes. Well, now they were acquainted. What next?

She vaguely remembered that she should pat it on the stomach as she sat down, hooking her left leg inside the cow's right back leg so it couldn't kick her. It might knock her over if it decided to kick up a fuss, but it wouldn't break anything.

"I know it's not your fault," she muttered as she perched herself uncomfortably on the short stool and tried to get things situated. First she had to get the big silver bucket between her knees, and then she had to get herself half under the cow. "Nope, it's not your fault. But you see, I have this thing about cows."

Gingerly, she reached for the closest teat and pulled down experimentally. She gritted her teeth. She didn't even like the feel of a cow. "Just don't like cows. Never did."

Wap. The cow's tail shot out and smacked her. It was cold and hard, and it stung, even through her sweater.

"I guess I'd better keep the insults to myself, huh, Bossy?"

"Her name's Cher."

She looked up, startled. Finn was lounging in the doorway to the milking shed, grinning at her. "Cher is a dopey name for a cow," she told him, trying to maintain her dignity. It was difficult in this position.

He lifted his gorgeous shoulders in a shrug. "I didn't name her."

"You have a habit of not naming things, don't you?"

He ignored her question, instead posing one of his own. "How are you doing out here?"

"Okay." Dumb answer, but what was she supposed to say? "What are you doing here, anyway? Checking up on me?"

He smiled. "Maybe I was checking to make sure you were still here."

"Here, as in the milking shed? Or here, as in Heavenly Acres?"

He shrugged. "Either."

She glanced up at him curiously. "Did you think I'd leave?"

"You were hot enough to get out of here before."

"Maybe I've changed my mind."

His blue eyes flicked her up and down as she sat awkwardly on the small stool. "Now why would you do a thing like that?"

"I don't know. Why would I?"

His eyes held hers as he played his cat-and-mouse game. She suddenly realized she wasn't doing a whole lot of milking at the moment. Studiously avoiding Finn's hot gaze, she concentrated on ol' Cher.

Her hands felt clumsy on the cow's ponderous teats, but she kept pulling and squeezing, as a slow stream of milk began to spatter into the bottom of the bucket. She'd totally lost her rhythm, but she guessed she was managing all right. Especially since she was under Finn's watchful eye, enough to make anyone a little jumpy.

She glanced over at him, and she couldn't help but notice that he was staring suspiciously at the easy motions of her hands. Oops. She wasn't supposed to know how to do this, was she?

"Oh, dear," she said loudly, purposely letting up with her right hand and directing the left one to spill half in and half out of the bucket. "I thought I was getting the knack of this. I don't know what I'm doing wrong."

Cher let out with another swipe of her tail, and Angie jumped. "Ow. That thing hurts. This cow doesn't like me, does she?"

"Here, let me help," Finn offered, in his best stern and serious voice.

Normally, she would've bristled at the very suggestion. She liked to do things her own way. But this time... Well, it wouldn't hurt her cover if he thought she was a klutz with cows. Besides, it was pretty fun pulling the wool over Finn's eyes.

He bent down closer, looking over her shoulder. "You need to... Here."

His hand covered hers as he knelt behind her, leaning in and around her. Angie tried not to notice, tried not to bend in a little closer as he spoke.

"Curl your fingers around like this," he told her, in the gentlest, kindest voice she'd ever heard. "Then just squeeze down with your thumb. Yeah, like that."

"Am I doing okay?" She released her hold on the bucket just so Finn would have to reach down and rearrange it. She smiled to herself. It was fun being naughty.

"You're doing just fine," he assured her.

She'd had this lesson before, as a child, but never like this. Not with Finn Sheridan breathing in her ear, holding her hand firm on the underside of a cow, brushing the whole side of his arm against her. She didn't know what her hand was doing, but he kept murmuring encouraging words and she kept pulling and squeezing. She could hear the splash of the milk in the pail, so they must be doing something right.

To her way of thinking, they were doing a lot of things right. His breath puffed hot and soft against her cheek, and his hand over hers was warm and strong. His other hand rested comfortably at her waist, and she felt protected, cherished. It was only an illusion, but a nice one.

"Finn," she whispered, closing her eyes, leaning into him, letting the milking fend for itself.

"Angel," he whispered back, close enough to nibble her ear.

The dribble of milk petered out. All she could hear was the sound of Finn's breathing. This was torture. She was trapped between him and the cow. Nowhere to run, nothing to be done but just...

"Whoa," he said abruptly, as she threatened to tumble backward off the stool and into his arms.

"Oh, dear," she murmured, smiling up at him, full of mischief. It was fun being bad. "Is the lesson over?"

"I think you can handle it just fine by yourself now." Setting her on the stool, he stood up and backed away a step, brushing straw off the knees of his jeans.

"Now why did you do that?" she asked. "We were doing so well."

"I'm trying to be a gentleman, Angel." He gave her a dark look. "But you are sorely provoking me."

"Sorry," she said brightly. "Guess I'd better get back to the milking, huh?"

"Yeah, I guess." His gaze narrowed as he watched her quickly work the front bags of the udder. He edged in a little closer, not too far from Cher's front leg. "You're a pretty darned fast learner, aren't you?"

"Oh, am I?" All innocence, she looked up at him and pointed the right front teat up as far as it would go, still squeezing. She'd planned on splashing a little milk on Finn's leg, just for fun. She hadn't planned on sending a steady stream right at his . . . crotch.

The look on his face was priceless. She couldn't help laughing out loud. "I hit you in . . . Gee, I'm sorry. I didn't mean to—"

"Think you're real funny, don't you?" he asked, advancing on her.

"No, I—"

But he hauled her up off that stool and into his arms before she got out another syllable.

"Real funny."

She was wiggling and laughing, but he wouldn't put her down, not until he got her way over on the other side of the shed, up against the wall.

"What are you going to do?" she asked, gasping for breath between bursts of laughter. "You're not properly equipped to shoot back. You're not packing a cow, are you, pardner?"

The idea of Finn brandishing a cow at her struck her as so funny she started to laugh all over again, until the hot, dangerous look on his face stopped her in mid-guffaw. "Why are you—?" she began, but this time his mouth cut her off.

His embrace was hard around her as he brought his lips down to cover hers. It was a harsh, steamy kiss, nasty and mean, and she wrapped her arms around his neck and opened her mouth to the assault.

His tongue swept her, his whole mouth devoured her, and she felt shock waves trip through her body.

"Whoa," she said, pulling away to breathe.

His eyes were alight with blue fire. "You're the one who wanted it."

"That was before I knew what it would be like. Whoa," she said again. She was still reeling.

"I tried to be a gentleman," he said calmly. "But you shot me."

"You deserved it."

"So did you."

She couldn't help smiling at him. He looked so damned pleased with himself. "Do I deserve it again?" she asked coyly.

But the fire in his eyes dimmed. "I don't think it's a good idea to get into this habit."

"Why not?" The mood had changed swiftly, and she was disappointed. When Finn offered no response, Angie broke the silence herself. "So you kissed me. It's not the end of the world."

"Look, I'm sorry."

"But why?"

"This can't happen." He raked a hasty hand through his hair. "You're under my protection. I don't make moves on the people under my roof."

"But I'm different."

"I'm not." His lips curved into a thin smile. "I could get real attached to having a woman like you around. And that's not good."

"Attached?" The very idea took her breath away. Finn, attached to her. The notion was as sweet as honey. "Not good?"

"You're a runaway, Angel," he reminded her. "And runaways keep running."

It was bleak and to the point. As well as completely true. The reality of her situation with Lance and Bibi and the Department of Housing Affairs came crashing back to earth. Finn was right. She had no business toying with him, or letting him under her skin, when she was just another problem child on the run as far as he was concerned.

"You're right," she told him, edging around him and heading back to her milkmaid stool. "So I guess I'd better finish my chore before Zero comes out here with a whip."

"Right." Softly, he added, "Oh, and Angel, keep the milk in the bucket this time, will you?"

"I'll try," she said sweetly. But when she took a gander at the big wet spot on the front of his pants, she knew there was mischief in her eyes.

HE COULD HEAR the sound of her laughter, coming from the basement. She was down there, playing at arts and crafts with some of the kids, and she was laughing. High and sweet, it sounded like the tinkling of bells.

It was driving him crazy.

Finn leaned way back in his office chair, staring intently at the picture of Abraham Lincoln's boyhood home on his free calendar from the feed store. But he wasn't focusing on the log cabin or even the now-defunct month of November. In his mind's eye, he was contemplating the puzzle he called Angel.

City girl, she'd told him. *Never been on a farm before in my life.*

So how did she come back with all those eggs? She hadn't asked what to put them in or how to spot the henhouse, just grabbed the egg basket off a hook and barged out there as if she had ESP and radar, both operating at the same time.

And then there was the cow. She hadn't been a pro with old Cher, but she sure hadn't been a novice, either. And he'd swear she'd shot him with milk on purpose, even though she'd sworn it was an accident. Her aim was too accurate to be accidental.

Finn shook his head. He'd bet the farm she was no city girl.

Frowning, he tipped even farther back in the chair. "So she's lying through her teeth," he muttered. "But why?"

As he stood up suddenly, his chair squeaked loudly in protest. He smacked at it with the flat of his hand. "Who is she? And why is she here?"

He knew he was getting curious, too curious for his own good. His policy dictated that Angel, like every other resident of Heavenly Acres, had a right to her privacy, and he had reminded himself of that fact a hundred times in the past few days.

He had no right to ask her questions, and she had no obligation to tell him anything. But the mystery was making him crazy.

"Why her?" he asked himself. A hundred or so kids had passed through the farm in the three short years of its operation, and he hadn't even been tempted to pry or to press for details of their lives. Not once. "Why her?"

But he knew the answer. She was a full-grown woman, not a kid, with a fully formed body and mind, and a unique ability to penetrate his defenses, to challenge his rules and his complacency. She'd come blasting in his door, socking him right in the gut, a living, breathing reminder that life was still out there, even if he was hiding in here.

She was a pain in the butt, and she felt like nobody's business wrapped in his arms. God, if he could only forget the feel of her.

"Too late," he told himself angrily. "You should've thought of that before you kissed her."

He could hear her on the basement stairs now, laughing and talking as she and the kids headed for the front door. "Finn, I'm taking your jacket," she called out to the closed door of his office, but he said nothing, even though he suddenly knew he didn't want her inside his clothes.

The front door slammed, and the happy little group tripped across the yard toward the paint shed. He had a clear view of their progress from his office window; even from this distance, he could see the sparkle in her eyes. He could also see the snug backside of her jeans, the too-long sleeves of her leather jacket—*his* jacket—

and the flutter of her long blond curls in the chilly December breeze.

His mouth went dry with sudden longing. "It's been too long," he whispered. Too long since he'd held a woman, too long since he'd heard a woman's laugh, too long since he'd felt the stirrings only a woman could start.

She was driving him crazy.

As he stared, captivated, she bent to help Derek carry his art project into the shed. Her hair spilled over onto her face, and she shook her head with good-natured annoyance, holding back the tangled mass with one hand while she reached for Derek's artwork with the other. She was beautiful, graceful, awkward—all at the same time.

Frowning, she held up the plywood animal Derek had been struggling with, turning it this way and that. Finn could tell she was trying hard to figure out exactly what it was. It looked like a skunk to him, but then he had more experience with the kids and the lawn ornaments they sold at craft fairs to make money. Comprehension dawned—her face practically glowed with it—as she beamed down at Derek and the skunk. If he hadn't known better, Finn would've sworn the sun was shining on this gloomy winter's day.

And then inside the shed they swept, Angel and Derek and the others, safely out of Finn's line of vision.

"Thank God," he said with conviction.

Safely out of his sight, and also out of the house. Now that she was occupied inside the paint shed, he knew what he had to do, what he'd been tussling with all morning.

"No," he declared angrily. "You don't go spying on people. It's against the rules, damn it."

But he was already on his way out of the office and up the stairs to her room—*his* room. It smelled like her now, like it wasn't his at all, and everywhere he looked she'd left her mark. It was nothing outrageous; she was as neat as a pin with her personal things. But still, he caught the glimmer of golden hairs wound into her hairbrush on the dresser, the faint scent of sweet shampoo clinging to a discarded towel tossed over a chair, and the subtle imprint of her personality in the way little pillows had been collected from other parts of the house and arranged prettily on her bed. The kitchen cat was sleeping on the bed, as if Angel had arranged that, too, for the coziest possible look.

Finn shook his head. Even the cat was defecting. The darned thing had never slept on the bed when it was his.

He picked up a little square pillow, something a teenage girl who'd passed through the farm a year or so ago had made out of calico and crisscrossed ribbons. Raising it to his nose, he caught the elusive scent of Angel, of her hair and her skin. It was crazy and stupid to stand around pressing his face into her pillow, but he couldn't resist.

What was it about her that seemed so fresh and untouched? He knew she was a runaway and very probably a troublemaker, but she looked and smelled and felt . . . like an angel.

With a muttered oath, he slammed the pillow back
on the bed, scaring the cat, who jumped off and hid
under the bed. But Finn turned his attention back to
the search he was supposed to be performing. Rif-
fling through the jumble of clothing in her duffel bag,
he felt like a rat all the way. He tried to tell himself she
might be dangerous to the well-being of the shelter,
and he had to know what she was up to just in case,
but he knew it was a joke even as he thought it.

"Oh, Lord," he moaned, holding up a tiny pair of
panties. They were pale aqua, no more than a snip of
lace attached to a satin ribbon.

"Oh, Lord," he said again. His mind conjured up
a full-blown picture of Angel, wearing nothing but
those scanty panties, and his body responded immediately.

Angel... on the bed, leaning back into the pillows
with a come-hither smile. He'd join her, pull her to
him, strip off those damn panties, and...

"Oh, Lord."

He dropped the panties back into the bag, as if his
fingers were on fire. If they weren't, the rest of him
was. Quickly, savagely, he zipped the duffel bag shut
and rammed it back in the closet.

Hastily, he raked both hands through his hair. He
felt like running out of the bedroom before things got
any worse. But he reminded himself that it was his
bedroom in the first place, and he could tear it apart
with his bare hands if he damned well pleased. Nonetheless, if he was going to search her belongings, he
needed something a lot less intimate than her underwear.

"Fur coat," he mumbled. It seemed safe enough, especially since she hadn't worn it since that first day. There it was, hanging neatly in the closet, but a rapid search of the pockets turned up absolutely nothing except for an empty bag of pork rinds. Not much to make of that, except maybe that she had questionable taste in snacks.

Now what? She'd succeeded in scorching him when she wasn't even in the same room, and he hadn't found out a damn thing yet.

"The purse," he muttered. He remembered the hideous alligator handbag from when he'd picked her up in Champaign. If she had IDs, he knew that's where they'd be.

Still feeling antsy, he spared a glance out the window, but everything looked okay in the paint shed. Of course, if she did happen to venture upstairs, he could say he was getting more clothes—it was, after all, his room—but he hated the idea that she'd know he was pawing around. He was supposed to be above that kind of nonsense.

"You're not above anything anymore," he said snidely, reaching for her purse where it was lying on the corner of the dresser. With every heartbeat, his case of guilt increased, but he wasn't turning back now.

Her purse wasn't as neat as the rest of her stuff. In fact, it was brimming over with pens and tissues and meaningless scraps of paper. Thankfully, there was no birth control or anything else to make him wonder what she'd been doing and who she'd been doing it with before she came to Heavenly Acres.

The first thing he saw of any interest was an unused train ticket from Chicago to Seattle. One side was torn off, as if the part that had brought her to Chicago had been collected by a conductor somewhere. Too bad. Her destination didn't tell him anything, but her point of origin might have. At least he could be pretty sure she hadn't started out in Chicago. But why hadn't she used the ticket to Seattle? And how had she ended up in Champaign?

"That's what I call a bad sense of direction."

Carefully, he lifted her wallet out of the purse, unfolding it and poking inside. No pictures. As in no pictures of husbands or kids. He breathed a little easier, but his fingers suddenly became awkward as he pulled out her driver's license. For the first time, he'd know who she was. By prying and sneaking around behind her back, he'd know. Did he really want to do this?

Yes, he did. Grimly, he abandoned his ethics and examined the license.

"Contessa Bibi von Kronenburg?" he said doubtfully. "You gotta be kidding."

Worse yet, it was an international driver's license, supposedly from Ruritania, whatever that was. It sounded vaguely familiar, like it was from a Marx Brothers' movie or something.

"Bogus," he decided, putting it back in the wallet.

And then his fingers hit a passport. "Ruritania" and an official-looking coat of arms were stamped in gold on the outside of the dark blue leather folder. Maybe it was a real place after all, but he was still doubtful.

Contessa Bibi again, he discovered, as he flipped the thing open. His eyes narrowed at the beautiful blonde in the fuzzy passport photo. The hair was right, but it wasn't Angel. By now, he knew Angel's features well enough to be very sure it wasn't the same woman, not even with plastic surgery. Even blurred, Contessa Bibi's eyes held a childish, petulant expression, and her pretty little mouth was curved into a spoiled pout. Angel's gaze was more guileless, yet more intelligent, and she couldn't have manufactured that dopey expression if she'd tried.

He tapped the passport against his leg, more perplexed than ever. If Angel wasn't Contessa Bibi von Kronenburg, then who was she? And why was she carrying someone else's passport?

"She's running from something dangerous," he mused. "Or maybe someone dangerous. And it's got to be pretty damn ugly, or she wouldn't need fake ID."

But if she were desperate enough to buy bogus identification, which didn't come cheap or easy, wouldn't she have come up with something better than this loony tunes stuff? Or maybe she'd stolen the IDs along with the fur coat. Maybe they both belonged to the real Contessa von-whatever, and Angel had ripped off the whole shot.

What kind of jam could she have been in to be that desperate? His stomach turned over as he considered Angel caught in trouble so deep, so perilous, that she'd deal with criminals to buy or steal counterfeit IDs.

Out of the corner of his eye, Finn caught the motion of the door of the paint shed sliding open. Too bad. He hadn't had a chance to go through the whole purse yet, but it was too late to fuss about it. Swiftly, he moved to put all of her things back where he'd found them and get out of there before anybody caught him. As he quietly shut the door to the bedroom and slipped back down to his office, his brain was clicking right along.

Theft? Murder? What would it take to make Angel run and hide? He didn't want to think it, but the idea came unbidden. Pictures or no pictures, maybe she'd had a boyfriend. A violent boyfriend. Angel with someone who'd hurt her.... It made him sick. And what if the trouble she was running from was an abusive husband? His fists tightened as he pictured himself strangling the life out of anyone who'd hurt Angel.

"Holy hell," he said to himself. With a sense of horror, he realized that it wasn't just curiosity or even suspicion he was experiencing. He was also feeling protective. Very protective. Deep in his heart, he was thinking he could help her, fix up her life into a real bowl of cherries, if he only knew what her story was. It was a bad sign.

"A very bad sign," he told himself wearily.

"Finn?" Zero stuck his head around the door. "Are you in there talking to yourself?"

"Of course not. Just getting some work done." He pretended to be checking out the notations on his Land of Lincoln calendar.

"Finn?" Zero asked again.

He turned toward the kid. "What?"

"That's last month—on the calendar. You need to switch it to December."

Swearing under his breath, he tore off November and the log cabin and smashed the old month inside one fist. Then he found a wan smile for Zero. "December it is. Did you need something else?"

"Okay, well, yeah. Are you going into town any time soon? I wanna come along, get some stuff, you know?"

Finn made up his mind on the spot. He had friends at the Champaign Police Department who might be able to fill in a few blanks where Angel was concerned. It was risky, but he had no doubt he could handle it if the cops got suspicious. No way in hell he'd turn her in, even if she'd done something terrible. No, he'd handle it himself. But he had to know.

"Yeah," he told Zero. "I need to go right now, as a matter of fact."

If you get too pushy or too involved, you and your shelter won't last five minutes, the gentle voice of Father Maguire reminded him.

But he forced himself to ignore the voice of reason. He hated breaking Father Maguire's rules—rules that had turned him around from a no-account street punk into an adult with a mission in life—but it was too late now. Much too late. He'd invaded her privacy, so his principles were already shot to hell. How much worse could it be to ask a few questions, put out some feelers?

Ignoring the cloud of disquiet already settling around his shoulders, Finn grabbed a different coat and felt in his pocket for his keys. "Let's get out of here before I change my mind."

Chapter Six

Angie didn't know a thing about lawn ornaments, but she was having a great time faking it. She would never have believed it could be this much fun to be mindless and silly. Her problems seemed to be stuck safely outside Heavenly Acres, with nothing around to cause even a twinge of anxiety.

"Angel?" Derek asked softly, pulling on her sleeve. "Sunk got blue eyes?"

"Skunk, dodo," retorted his older sister, a pale slip of a thing named Layla. With the back of one hand, she swiped long wisps of brown hair out of her eyes. "Skunk, not sunk."

"Sunk," he insisted.

Angie shushed them both. Derek's paint job looked very little like a skunk or any other animal known to man, but why spoil it? "I knew what he meant, so that's okay. Sure, it can have blue eyes. Why not?"

As the small boy ran off to find blue paint, Layla crossed thin arms over her chest and frowned. "That's bad for him," she said sullenly. "You shouldn't treat him like a baby. He's not a baby, you know."

Angie shrugged, smiling. She'd already learned that the best way to deal with the young denizens of the shelter was simply to grin and keep going. If she steered clear of Finn completely, not to mention Zero and his sulky pals, she could concentrate on the younger kids who were thrilled just to have somebody—anybody—pay attention. And she did just fine. In fact, she did pretty darned good for somebody who wasn't crazy about kids.

It was weird, she decided, to be growing into a different person entirely. Gone were Angie Marie Boone's sedate suits and high heels. Gone were the prim hairdo and the elegant pearls. Now she wore the same pair of jeans every day, and her hair was going wild. She hadn't had a cup of coffee in almost a week, and she was stuffing her face with things like pancakes and sausage, and potatoes and gravy, for goodness' sake. She was an Angie even she didn't recognize.

"He's not a baby," Layla repeated stubbornly.

"Of course he's not. He's, what, four or five?"

Layla slapped a brush full of black paint down on the table near her plywood pig. "Shows what you know. My brother is nine."

"Nine?" Angie gasped. But he was so tiny, and he spoke so poorly. "But, Layla . . ." She tried not to act too shocked. "How old are you?"

"Eleven," she said proudly.

Could Layla be lying? She didn't look more than seven or eight. Angie knew she wasn't supposed to pry, but she couldn't help herself. "How long have you been here?"

"I dunno." The girl shrugged her narrow shoulders. "I guess a year or something. It was my birthday when our ma dumped us at the mall, and then it was my birthday again a while ago, so that would have to be a year, wouldn't it?"

Angie didn't know what to say. Finn had called the kids at the shelter runaways and throwaways, and Derek and his sister clearly fit into the second bunch.

"So she just left us at the mall," Layla continued. "Me and Derek were sitting there waiting for our ma to come back and pick us up, only she didn't. So Finn took us instead."

She'd thought her own problems with Lance and the housing department was the stuff of tragedy, but it seemed like small potatoes after hearing Layla's story. Dumped at the mall? Picked up by a stranger and stuck in a totally new place?

"Thank goodness for Finn," she said softly. For the first time, she thought of him as a knight in shining armor. He wasn't at all the type, but he was doing the work, and that was what counted, wasn't it?

"Uh-huh. We're glad Finn took us." Layla set the finished pig aside to dry, and then picked up a silhouette of a fat lady bending over. "I think these are so gross, don't you?"

It was a relief to change the subject. "Yes, I do. Why don't you paint something else?" Sticking the whole pile of fat ladies out of sight, Angie offered Layla a cutout of a cat. "How about this? You can make it look like the kitty in the kitchen."

"Okay." Smacking her lips and squinting at the cat, Layla started to hum something tuneless, and Angie took the opportunity to supervise the other kids in the paint shed. Except for a small spat over who got to use the red first and a dangerous puddle from a spilled cup of purple, everything was okay if a bit heavy on the paint fumes.

As Angie slid back the door to the shed to let in some fresh air, she cast a surreptitious glance over at the window to Finn's office. She couldn't see him, but she wondered idly whether he was in there and what he was doing. And how he found the energy, day in and day out, to deal with little kids lost like Derek and Layla. So much responsibility for one man.

"I wonder if he ever takes a day off," she whispered. "I wonder if he's ever lonely."

"Are you talking to me?" Layla asked.

"No, just mumbling to myself."

"Oh, well, I thought maybe you were talking about Finn." Layla gazed up at her with an eager expression. "He's so cool, isn't he?"

Quickly, Angie busied herself mixing colors in little cups. "Is he?"

"Way cool. Everybody is crazy about Finn!" The little girl's eyes got brighter as she leaned in closer. "He's really rich, did you know that?"

"Oh?" She tried to pretend that she was only vaguely interested, but the truth was, she was eaten up with curiosity. Of course, she was trying to bear in mind that Layla's information could hardly be considered reliable. This rich thing, for example. Maybe Layla thought anybody who had a leather jacket was rich.

"He's from Philo...something."

"Philadelphia?"

Layla nodded vigorously. "Yeah, yeah, that." Dropping her voice, she laid a hand on Angie's arm, as if they were the best of pals. The gesture was strangely similar to one Angie had shared with Gretchen millions of times at lunches when the gossip was getting good.

"So," Layla confided meaningfully, "his mom and dad were really rich, really rolling in it, richer than anybody you ever met, richer than Scrooge McDuck, that's what Zero said. And so Finn really hated their guts, but nobody knows why, not even Zero, but probably because they were so rich and mean, you know, like aristo-cats."

"Crats. Aristocrats," Angie corrected. Finn a Philadelphia aristocrat? Mr. Tough Guy with a silver spoon in his mouth?

"So he ran away from home, just like Zero. Isn't that cool?"

"Cool," Angie echoed. Against her better judgment, she was starting to get sucked into this story.

"And then he ek-scaped his evil parents." Layla's eyes kept getting bigger and bigger and her voice throbbed with excitement. "And he got in bad trouble, real bad, like the cops or something, and this nice guy who ran a shelter took him in, Father Somebody, and he saved Finn and made him have a shelter of his own. But Finn never went back to Philo...Phila...you know, that place. Totally cool, huh?"

"Totally," Angie said thoughtfully.

She wished she knew whether or not to believe Layla. The girl's gossipy story actually did seem to fit

Finn, in an odd way, but it did little to satisfy Angie's curiosity. In fact, it only made her more intrigued.

"Finneas Augustus McKinley Sheridan, that's his real name," Layla said happily. "It's on this thing on his wall in his office, like an award, for making Heavenly Acres and being a point of light. That's what it says. Finneas Augustus McKinley Sheridan. You can tell he used to be a rich-o, 'cause that's the kind of name those people have."

Angie could imagine Finn at seventeen or eighteen, already with a chip on his gorgeous shoulders, Rebel Without a Cause, hanging out on street corners, getting into trouble, making all the girls swoon with young lust....

She shook her head. Better concentrate on something else.

Could Finn really have been a teenage runaway picked up and saved by some version of Father Flanagan and *Boys' Town?* Maybe Zero had seen the movie and adopted it for everyone's favorite mystery man.

"It's true," Layla swore solemnly. "Every word. This old guy came to visit at the farm, that Father guy, and he told Zero the whole story. Finn never told anybody, because he didn't want us to know about him being rich and stuff. Because all he has to do is go back to his mom and dad and they'll give him all the money, but Finn doesn't want to, because," she finished up triumphantly, "he'd rather stay here with us."

"That's really interesting, Layla." *Finn Sheridan, a hero for our times,* Angie thought cynically. Poor but honest. A real Cinderella story, except Cinderella was a man who wore a torn T-shirt and too-tight jeans. "Oh, stop it," she muttered. "You're just jealous because he's on the level and you're not."

"Huh?"

"Nothing, Layla. Umm, why don't you put away your cat and we'll see about getting some lunch?" Angie had had enough salacious gossip about Finn for one morning; she was already fascinated with the man, and Layla's White Knight fairy tales only made it worse. "You kids finish up and wash your hands," she called out sternly. "I'm going into the house. Put away all the paint before you come in. Got it?"

She got a few nods in return, and she took off for the house, alternately dreading and anticipating seeing Finn. Would she be able to treat him the same now that she knew his life story? And if she acted any differently, would he know she knew?

It was all so complicated. "I'll have to act nonchalant," she said out loud. "I can do that." But how? The way he'd turned his back on his past and turned his life around, it made him sound so selfless, so noble, he probably expected people to bow down and pay homage whenever they saw him.

"Oh, Angie," she whispered as she strode purposefully into the empty kitchen, "he's just a man, not a saint."

"What did you say?"

Oh, God, it was him. There he was, right behind her, slipping through the door before it even had a chance to close. How could she have thought for one minute that he was "just" a man?

Finn Sheridan wasn't ordinary. Wearing the usual jeans and a T-shirt, with a denim jacket slung over one shoulder, he carried that whole moody, careless attitude that made her want to scream and throw herself at him, both at the same time. Arrogant, yes. Saintly? Ha.

In the flesh, he didn't seem the least bit like a saint. No, not Finn Sheridan. He was too real and too vital, dripping masculinity as casually as he dropped his coat on a kitchen chair. It was as if Thor had shown up at the back door, thunderbolts in hand, and asked her if she wanted to take a ride in his chariot.

"I . . . uh," she mumbled, backing into the table.

"What's with you?" He sent her a cautious look as he edged around her and dropped a thick packet of papers on the kitchen table. "Is something wrong?"

"Uh, no, of course not. You just surprised me."

"I seem to have a habit of doing that."

"Yes, you do." *Act nonchalant,* she ordered herself. "So," she said bravely, "where have you been?"

"Went into town," he said gruffly. He inclined his thumb at the stack of papers on the table. "Picked up the mail and a newspaper. Thought I'd catch up on current events."

"Oh, that's nice."

And then the word penetrated. *Newspaper.* She hadn't seen a newspaper in days, not since the man on the train, the one who was sure he recognized her face. Heavens to Betsy. Her face was probably plastered all over Finn's newspaper.

And there he was, angling around to the table, browsing through the packet of envelopes, fiddling with the letters, only inches away from pulling out that newspaper and exposing her face to the harsh light of day.

"Wait," she cried, sliding in between him and the table, slapping down the stack of mail with her hand.

He held his ground. "Well? What is it?"

"I have a, uh, problem," she improvised. Alarm bells were clanging in her brain. All she could think of was that she *had* to keep him away from that newspaper. So she sat on it. Sliding back onto the table an inch or two, she planted herself right on top of the damned thing.

"Well, what is it?" he asked impatiently.

"You," she said quickly. It was all she could think of, especially since he was practically in her lap.

"Me? What did I do?"

"Everything," she said with a heartfelt sigh. That was certainly true enough. Everything about him was a problem and a dilemma.

"I don't know what you're talking about," he muttered, reaching around behind her and feeling for the newspaper, which just happened to be securely wedged under her bottom. His hand brushed and held the curve of her back pocket, testing the give of the paper, but she stayed where she was, blocking his access as firmly as she could. She bit her lip and held on, while her body started to feel like warm gelatin.

His eyes met hers, and she could read the wary interest there. His hand tickled the middle seam on the back of her jeans. She knew what he was up to. He thought if he touched her and teased her and sent her out of her mind, she'd give up and move. He was wrong. She bit down harder, not moving an inch.

Finally, after groping around for several long moments, purposely making her crazy, he gave up and asked, "Could you please move? I'd like to have my paper if it's okay with you."

"No, it's not okay with me," she said stiffly.

She was feeling rather miffed that she'd stuck her derriere and a whole lot of temptation right smack in the middle of his affairs and he hadn't even cared. She'd made the first move, hadn't she? He could've pushed her back on the table and kissed her until they were both mindless. But all he wanted was his stupid newspaper!

"Finn, will you please pay attention to me?" she demanded. "I'm trying to discuss something important and you're ignoring me."

"I'm not ignoring you," he said darkly. "I'm trying, but I'm not succeeding in any way, shape or form."

Well, that was gratifying. "So will you stop whining about your newspaper and listen to me?"

"I'm listening," he growled. "You're not saying a damn thing."

"Well, it's just . . . not easy to talk about."

"Try me."

Okay, now what was she going to come up with? She needed to sidetrack him long enough to dispose of the newspaper, which meant getting him out of the kitchen. But so far, all she'd succeeded in doing was pulling him even closer.

"So?" he prompted. "What did you want to discuss with me?"

She reached up and carefully fingered the edge of his strong jaw. "Finn," she said softly, gazing deep into his blue, blue eyes, "do you ever get lonely out here, all by yourself?"

"Why?" He caught her hand and held it away from his face. "Are you feeling lonely, Angel? Is this about you, not me?"

"Maybe."

"Kids not enough to keep you company, huh?"

"Are they for you?"

He opened her palm, cradling her hand in his, and then he brought the whole thing to his lips. Slowly, softly, he pressed a kiss into the center of her palm. Angie's breath caught in her throat.

"No," he murmured. "The kids aren't enough. Is that want you wanted to hear?"

She swallowed. "I'm not sure."

"You better get sure, Angel. You're treading a dangerous path with a dangerous man."

"I think I'm perfectly safe with you."

"Then you're not as smart as I thought you were."

His eyes seemed darker and more heated now, and she believed him when he said he was a dangerous man. Dangerous to her, anyway. But she didn't care.

"Sometimes," she whispered, "it's hard not to push you. You're so perfect, Finn, so selfless, so saintly. It's hard not to want to puncture that perfection, to see where the man is under the facade."

"Don't push too hard," he warned. "You may not like what you find."

"I think I'd like it just fine."

He smiled then, a slow, mocking smile, and he reached down and lifted her chin with one finger. Dipping his head down, he brushed his lips against hers, so softly she wasn't sure she hadn't imagined the whole thing.

She wanted to press closer, to deepen the kiss, but Finn kept his distance. When she tried to pull him down into her mouth, he drifted away, feathering her cheeks and her nose and the corners of her lips with elusive, unsatisfying kisses.

"Finn, please," she tried.

But he shook his head. "I want to know what you're up to," he murmured.

"Up to?"

"With me. Why you're dancing around me, driving me crazy. What's in it for you?"

"You," she said softly. She hadn't thought about the answer. She was supposed to be a full-time liar now, so why did the truth come so easily? "Maybe all I want is you."

"No, you don't." Reluctantly, he drew away. "I'm nobody's prize."

"But everybody here has a piece of you."

"Not you," he told her gently. And then he kissed her again, less carefully, with a reckless burst of heat she knew they'd both regret later. "No, Angel, I'm still not convinced you're telling me the truth. When you're ready to tell me what this is all about, I'll be ready to listen."

Without warning, he turned and slipped out the back door, leaving her half on and half off the kitchen table, shaking like a leaf on an aspen tree.

Well, she'd gotten rid of him, hadn't she? Too bad she'd spilled her guts and made a fool of herself in the process.

"I told him I wanted him," she whispered, raising a hand to her flushed cheek. "He had to know already, but I'm not sure I did. What a stupid thing to do."

It was too late for recriminations now, wasn't it? He was gone, he'd turned her down once again, and she was feeling like a fool.

"Well, Angie," she said out loud, "you better quit mooning around and take care of business while you have the chance."

As quickly as she could manage, she peeled open the newspaper. Small comfort to see that she'd been right to safeguard it. There it was again, the same hideous picture and awful story. "Politico's Mistress" this time, instead of "sex kitten," but it hardly mattered.

Thank goodness she'd been lucky enough to intercept it. If Finn had seen this, he would've kicked her out so fast, her head wouldn't have had time to spin.

As she scanned it, she saw a picture and a reference to poor, innocent Gretchen and the FBI, and a whole lot of rhetoric about not stopping until Angie Marie Boone, the criminal of the century, was safely behind bars.

Clearly, this newspaper had to die. With a real sense of satisfaction, she crumpled the front page into a ball and scoped out the kitchen for some matches. And then she set Politico's Mistress ablaze in the kitchen sink. Once it was reduced to cinders, Angie drowned it all and sent it swirling down the drain.

And she was safe for the moment. Wasn't she?

"NOTHING?" FINN ASKED again. "Not one damn thing?"

There was silence on the other end of the receiver for several seconds.

"Mel, you still there?" he asked.

"Sorry, Finn," his friend from the police station shot back cheerfully. "It's nuts around this place today. We just had a punk hold up a drive-through window—on foot, do you believe it? Caught him a block away, still carrying the Burger Barn bag."

"I believe it," he returned, thinking of some of the kids who'd passed through the shelter. "So you got nothing on my pal Angel, right?"

"I got zip." Sergeant Melvin Sibley barked out a rough approximation of a laugh. "Usually you want us to stay out of your business, but now you want quick answers. Never happy, are you, Sheridan? Give me some fingerprints, a name, even a nice obvious scar might be nice, but, hey, I got nothing on any missing blonde or any stolen fur coat from the five-state area."

"Okay, well, keep your eyes open, will you? I'd give a lot to know where my newest runaway ran away from."

"I thought you didn't ask about that kind of thing," Sibley commented shrewdly. "They get a little older, you get a little more interested, huh?"

"Something like that."

"Later, Finn," the sergeant said abruptly. "Gotta go—they just brought in a couple of joyriders."

"Yeah, bye," he offered, although there didn't seem much point with a dial tone ringing in his ear. Carefully, he replaced the receiver, wishing he could get himself to back off this crazy obsession. But every time he saw her, it only got worse. He couldn't look at her, hear her voice, without it gnawing at his gut. *Who are you? What—or who—did you run from?*

"Finn?"

"Yeah?" Zero again. The kid had been dropping in and out of the office every five minutes for the past few days. What was going on there?

"Got a minute?"

"Sure." Finn pulled his chair around and straddled it, inclining a thumb at the side chair. "Sit," he ordered. "What's up?"

Zero's lips pressed together. "Her."

"Her?"

"You know, *her.*"

"Ah. Angel."

"Yeah."

"So what's the problem?"

"What's she doing here?" Zero demanded. "I mean, she's no kid. Why does she have to be here?"

"I'm not a kid. I'm here."

"Yeah, but you run the place, Finn. It's your place!"

"Floyd's not a kid."

Zero rolled his eyes. "Cut the jokes, Finn. Floyd is an old stooge and he don't live here, anyway. He ain't been here for a couple weeks—must be making some other poor dopes learn how to cut bunnies out of plywood, huh?''

Finn allowed himself a small smile. Personally, he was rather fond of Floyd, a retired industrial arts teacher with an ex-marine attitude and haircut. But none of the boys ever seemed to warm up to gruff, nononsense Floyd, even though he was a wonder with a band saw and a tool belt.

''So Floyd doesn't count as an adult, either, then?'' he inquired casually.

''Not like her,'' Zero returned.

''What's she doing that gets to you?'' he asked. *Everything,* his heart answered. He hoped Zero's reasons were different from his own.

''It's not me,'' Zero mumbled. ''It's the little kids, mostly Derek and Layla. She's all mushy and nice to them, and I just think, well, you know, it's not the way we do things around here.''

Finn leaned back in his chair. He thought he had an inkling as to what this was really about, but he was going to have to wait till Zero got around to the point. ''So you'd rather she wasn't nice to Derek and Layla?''

''They could get the wrong idea—that she's gonna be around. But she won't stay. I mean, she won't stay, will she?''

It wasn't a question he cared to pursue. Would she stay? Could he stand it if she did? Could he stand it if she didn't?

"I don't know, Zero. I just don't know." Noting the sulky expression that answer brought to Zero's face, Finn asked, "What's the look for?"

"You." Zero shifted around defiantly. "You got a thing for her, don't you?"

Aw, hell. He didn't want to deal with this. "Nope," he said tersely. "I haven't got anything for anybody."

"I ain't buying it, Finn," Zero persisted. "Are you...?" But he broke off, looking even surlier and more frustrated than before.

"Spit it out."

"Are you two makin' it?"

Finn choked. He hadn't expected that. Exerting control over his desire to knock some sense into Zero, Finn stood quietly, looming over the boy. "I won't take that from you or anybody else. You hear me, Z.? It's a cheap shot. And I'm not going for it."

"Okay, okay. I'm sorry." But he glanced up from under his droopy lids. "So why don't you just boot her butt out of here?"

Finn sighed. "Well, that's putting it right on the line."

"She doesn't belong here. We never had any *ladies* before." The boy narrowed his dark eyes. "I mean, who is she, and what's she doing here, anyway? Have you asked her?"

"We don't ask questions like that, kid. You know that."

"Yeah, I know. Rule number four—nobody has to say anything about where they came from or why they left unless they want to," Zero recited in a mocking tone. "But couldn't we make an exception?"

"I don't make exceptions when it comes to the rules." God, what a hypocrite he was becoming. He broke the rules every time he turned around when it came to Angel, but he couldn't admit it to the kid. Erosion, he thought. Erosion of his principles and the sanctity of his shelter. What next? Caffeine and cigarettes in every room? He allowed himself a bitter laugh.

"It ain't funny," Zero protested. "I think she's screwing up this whole place and you're letting her! She's in there right now reading Derek and Layla a bedtime story, like she was their mom or something. It's gross, Finn. Totally gross."

"Okay, I got the message. I'll talk to her about getting too attached to Derek and Layla, all right?" He frowned. "But none of this 'she doesn't belong here' stuff. Everybody's welcome. You know that."

"Yeah, awright." Still looking gloomy, Zero scuffled out of the room.

So she was reading bedtime stories, was she? Heavenly Acres was changing, and that's what Zero didn't like. No longer Finn's second-in-command, the kid had to share his authority now, as bit by bit, Angel ingratiated herself into the ebb and flow of their daily lives. She had just swept in and started taking things over. Like the lion's share of his attention, for one.

"I guess I'm going to have to talk to her," he said softly. It wasn't that he wasn't looking forward to it. No, he was looking forward to it a little *too* much.

Chapter Seven

Angel was snuggled into an overstuffed rocking chair in the living room, with Derek in her lap and Layla tipping onto her shoulder from the arm of the chair. As she read some sweet little story about ducks, her voice sounded soft and tender, lilting up and down with the characters she was playing. The light from a standing lamp spilled over her shoulder, casting a golden glow on the long waves of her hair, catching the tops of Derek and Layla's heads as they bent closer to hear the story.

Angel looked beautiful, vulnerable, and the kids looked more innocent and angelic than any who'd ever come through the doors of Heavenly Acres. It was precisely the kind of scene he'd never expected to see in his own home. It wasn't supposed to be this way—this cozy mother-and-child, bedtime story fantasy. Not in Finn Sheridan's hard world.

"Hell," he muttered. "It's a Hallmark card."

He didn't say anything within earshot, but she must have sensed his presence, because she stopped the story and glanced up. Neither spoke, as the silence in the room grew heavy and thick.

"Did you want something?" she asked finally.

"I want lots of things."

He regretted the words the moment they escaped him. Too flippant, too angry, too flirtatious, especially in front of the children. But he did mean them. Want? He was filled with wanting. Wife, kids, sheepdog, house in the suburbs—all those soft, sweet things he wasn't supposed to care about at all.

But mostly he just wanted Angel.

He wished to high heaven she had never raised the issue of wanting. But it was too late now. He wanted to wrap himself in her angel hair. He wanted to taste her open, wet mouth and run his fingers over her soft white skin. He wanted to press her down into his bed, to hold her above him in the moonlight, to feel her hair tangled across his chest. He wanted . . . all kinds of things he could never have.

He fought back the hunger.

"I need to talk to you," he said stiffly.

"Okay." She smiled down at the children tumbled into her lap. "I think they're asleep, though. Maybe you could carry them to bed, the way you took Derek the first night I got here."

"I don't think so." He shrugged, jamming his hands into the front pockets of his jeans. "I think they're faking it, anyway. Come on, guys, time to hit the road."

They didn't stir, but their frozen positions convinced him he was right. "Definitely faking it." Layla opened one eye a sliver. "I saw that," he said gruffly. "All right, that's it. Out of here, you two."

"Aw, gee, Finn," they chorused, but they scampered off her chair and back to the kitchen when he gave them a sterner look.

Alone. He shook his head to remind himself why he was here—not to be alone with Angel, but to make a few things clear.

Absently, he said, "I thought you were the one who wanted more discipline. Now I have to be the bad guy."

"Well, not with those two. They're sweethearts," she countered, rising from her chair and dusting off her jeans.

His eyes followed the movement of her pale fingers, splayed against the dark blue denim, drawing his attention to her rounded bottom and then her long, tight thighs, until he had to look away or go out of his ever-loving mind. Concentrating on a spot over her head, he hoped he could think clean thoughts and stay out of trouble.

"They don't need a heavy hand," she continued. "They're great kids, especially considering, you know, their mother. I don't know how a person could be that heartless." Her pretty features grew stern. "I could just strangle that woman. Can you imagine, dumping them at the mall?"

"Yeah, I can imagine," he returned sharply. "I picked them up."

"I know you know." She smiled bravely. "It's just so heart-breaking when you realize what those kids have been through."

"Life is like that," he said flatly.

She sent him a quick glance. "Well, not for Derek and Layla—not if I can help it."

"And how do you propose to help it?"

She shrugged. "Some attention, some kindness."

"That's what I wanted to talk to you about."

"I don't understand."

"Too much attention, too much kindness."

Her voice became confused. "Are you saying there's something wrong with being nice to a couple of love-hungry kids?"

"If it goes too far."

"But it isn't going too far," she insisted.

"The hell it's not," he said under his breath. He, better than anyone, knew just how deeply Angel was imbedded at Heavenly Acres.

"That's another thing," she said primly. "You just said 'hell,' and you do that a lot. I don't think all this swearing is good for the children."

"These kids have lived on the streets. You think they've never heard the word *hell?*"

"It can't be good for them," she insisted.

"What isn't good for them is getting too attached."

"To me?"

"To anybody." He ran an impatient hand through his hair. "You may not be around tomorrow—they may not be around tomorrow. Did you ever think about that?"

"Well, no, but—"

"This is a way station, Angel, not a home. It's for people with nowhere else to go. But everybody hits the road eventually. If you start acting like the Waltons, how do you leave? How do you handle it when you have to go, or when Derek and Layla's mother shows up and wants them back?''

''I wouldn't let her have them back.''

He tried not to smile. She actually thought she could stamp her little foot and right the world's wrongs. ''Angel,'' he said softly, ''the world doesn't work like that. You don't have a choice sometimes.''

''Well, if that day came, I would deal with it. Just like you would.''

''But you're nothing like me,'' he reminded her. Wherever she'd been, life had treated her well enough that she hadn't developed the scars or the protective shell the rest of them had. ''In some ways, Angel, you're more innocent than Derek.''

''Baloney,'' she shot back. ''And I'm glad I'm not like you, not getting attached, keeping to yourself, lonely and cold and cranky....''

So she thought he was cold and cranky. It stung more than he would've thought. ''If you'd been around here as long as I have, you'd know that you can't get too involved with any one kid,'' he said carefully. ''It doesn't work.''

''Oh, baloney!'' she said again. ''You're already attached, worse than I am.''

''I am not.''

She strode right up to him and poked a finger in his chest. ''You are so. You think I don't notice the way you are with Derek and Layla and even Zero? You love those kids, and it would break your heart if they left.''

He caught her by the shoulders. "Then I guess my heart's already broken," he said, gazing down at her. "Do you know how many kids have been in and out of here since I started this place? Do you know how many runaways I've seen?"

Some emotion he couldn't read—didn't want to read—rose in her eyes. "I'm sorry, Finn. I'm so sorry."

"Don't be." He clenched his jaw. "The last thing I want is you sorry for me."

"But how do you do it?"

"What?"

"Live here, all by yourself. Take them in and then lose them, one by one." Angel put her arms around him; he knew it was meant for comfort, but it didn't feel that way. "How can you take so much on yourself?"

He rested his head on top of hers, allowing himself to relax for the moment. "I don't think about it. I just do it."

"I guess I don't understand how you got here in the first place," she said softly. "I mean, I know the story, about your family out east and Father What's-his-name who took you in. So you're paying him back by carrying on the effort, is that it?"

He tensed. "How do you know about that?"

"Layla told me." Angel pulled back, watching him closely. "I didn't know it was a secret."

"It isn't." He exhaled slowly. "I just didn't expect you to know, that's all."

"Does it make a difference?"

He stared down at her soft green eyes, knowing that it did make a difference. But why?

I don't want you inside my head. I don't want you to know anything about my past. I don't want you to know me.

Damn it. He couldn't stand there, looking at her, watching her breasts rise and fall with each sweet breath. Abruptly, he turned, releasing her.

"It doesn't matter," he said after a moment. "Why should it?"

"Are you afraid I might figure out the real you? Is that it?" she asked, still gazing at him with that mixture of fascination and pity.

Pity. He couldn't stand it. Lightly, he offered, "It hardly seems fair that you should know my whole life story when I don't know anything about you."

But his challenge hung in the air, unanswered.

"I guess that means you don't want to tell me," he decided. "I guess you're afraid, too. Afraid I might figure out the real you."

"It's your rule, not mine," she reminded him. She was fiddling with the doily on the back of the chair, pointedly not looking at him. "I don't have to tell you anything, remember?"

He caught her hand, ending the fiddling. "You don't have to. I thought maybe you'd want to."

"I don't," she said flatly. She shook her head. "Is this how you get all the runaways to tell you their secrets? I've got to tell you—I'm not thrilled being treated like one of the kids."

A pause separated them for a long beat. "Is that what you think I do?"

She licked her lip. "Yes."

"If I treat you like a child," he said roughly, "it's only because I don't think of you as a child at all."

The mood shifted as abruptly as his tone. Between them, sympathy turned into something darker, smokier, more difficult to gauge. She caught her breath, exhaling unevenly, and he could read the same desire in her wild green eyes that he felt rising in himself. Her face was flushed and warm, and he couldn't resist raising a hand, grazing his knuckles against the softness of her cheek. After a long pause, as their eyes held, he whispered, "You're no child, Angel."

"Then treat me like what I am." Her voice was barely audible. "Like a woman."

Her lips were so close and so moist, so tantalizing. "We can't do this," he murmured, as he bent down and brushed his open mouth against hers. Just a touch, just a taste of what they could have if they'd only let it happen. "Against the rules."

"All wrong," she told him, winding her arms around his neck, lifting her body further into his embrace. "A terrible idea."

"Terrible," he echoed, nipping at her ear, trailing his lips along the curve of her neck, brushing soft kisses across her cheeks and her mouth. God, she was sweet and willing and warm. He wanted to resist, to push away and run, but there didn't seem to be any way in hell to do it.

"What are we doing?" he whispered.

"Something we shouldn't," she said hungrily, threading her small hands through his hair, pulling him down closer. "Something we can't."

He groaned, but there was no room for words. Her mouth was open and wet under his, hot and demanding. He plunged in with his tongue, blocking out his brain, as he fed off her little moan of desire, her tenderness, her eagerness to push him as far as he would go.

This wasn't a kiss; it was a battle of wills.

He slipped his hands down to the curve of her buttocks, settling her against the hot, tight pressure in his jeans, and she moaned into his mouth, rubbing up into him until he thought he might die from heat and hunger.

A few more seconds of this, and he'd have her down on the couch, stripped and naked and ready to love, before either of them knew what hit them.

"No," he managed. Fiercely, he framed her face with his hands as he pushed away, far enough to breathe, to think, to ask himself what in hell he thought he was doing.

"Angel," he said raggedly. But it was too late. He was no saint. Not him. At the moment, he was all man. And he wanted her more than he could say.

He fastened his lips to her, drinking her in. She tasted so sweet, so alive, and he knew it had been much too long since he felt that way.

Was it possible to have the things he'd always denied? No matter what she was running from, Angel was an innocent. He'd never been with an innocent.

"Angel," he said slowly, nuzzling her neck, pulling her to him fiercely, possessively. "Is this what you want?"

"Yes. No." She kissed him on the lips, quickly. "I don't know."

"If you don't know, why are you kissing me?"

She smiled, and he couldn't keep an answering grin from his own lips. "Maybe because I like it," she whispered. "Maybe because I like you."

"Maybe that's not very smart." But he kept kissing her, tangling a hand deep into her hair, trailing his lips over her forehead and her cheeks.

"I never said I was smart."

"Didn't you?"

She shook her head. "Not when it comes to you."

He rested his forehead on hers. "I can't believe this is happening again."

There was a pause, as Angel went still under him. "Again? Are you saying this has happened before?"

If he wanted a way out of this madness, it looked like he'd found it. Too bad he was past the point of looking for an escape. "Not exactly."

She took a breath and pushed away. "I think you'd better explain."

"Let's just say I used to have a weakness for damsels in distress."

"Damsels in distress?" She ran her hands through the hair at her temples, sliding it away from her face. "So it isn't me you're interested in. It's the fact that I'm in trouble."

"No, it's not like that," he tried, but he could see that she was hurt.

"Now I really feel like one of the kids. Although I guess you're trying to fix my problems in a different way."

"Please, Angel, don't—"

"Look, it's my own fault," she said hastily. "I'm the one who kept pressuring you. But if this has happened before, and if it's a problem for you, well, then, I'm not going to be the one to...you know."

"Angel, it's not your fault. I kissed you, remember?"

"But I didn't...I mean, I should've... Oh, hell, I don't know anything any more."

A wry smile lifted one side of his lips. "You said 'hell,' sweetheart. I thought it was against the rules."

"You're the one with all the rules," she said shakily. "Although this little episode has got to have broken every single one of them."

He raked a hand through his hair. "If it didn't, I'd better make up some new ones."

"I'm sorry," she whispered painfully.

"So am I." The words reverberated through his body, not quite reaching the ache deep inside. "So am I."

Angel sank into the armchair, fiddling with a long tendril of blond hair, still avoiding looking at him. "You said before that you weren't interested unless I told you who I was and all the rest."

"Yeah?"

"I can't, Finn. I just can't."

"Okay. I guess."

"So the rules are still the same. I really needed somewhere like this," she said softly, "where I could just kind of take refuge. I don't want to screw it up, all because I can't seem to, you know..."

"I know." He knew only too well. *Because I can't seem to keep my hands off you. Because I can't seem to stay away.* "Angel," he ventured, "I know you think whatever you ran away from is awful. Or who-ever." His jaw tightened. "But it's nothing I haven't heard before. If you could tell me about it, I might be able to help."

"You couldn't help."

"Are you sure?"

"Positive," she said softly.

What could it be? He couldn't imagine anything Angel could do that would even mildly shock him.

"Finn, I think maybe we should talk about this...situation." She sped up, as if she could only say it fast, or not at all. "If I'm going to stay, this can't happen again. You agree, don't you?"

"Yes. Absolutely."

"Okay, then." She breathed a sigh of relief. "Do I have your word?"

"Yes. Whatever you want."

"For the good of Heavenly Acres, we'll call a truce. No...fooling around."

"Whatever you want," he said again.

But deep in his heart, he knew it wouldn't last. There was something about the two of them that kept stirring up trouble. No matter how hard they tried, sparks would keep flying. And Angel would keep driving him crazy.

ANGIE WAITED UNTIL midmorning, when all the kids were busy wood-working with Floyd, and after Finn had gone into town to get supplies. Then she sneaked into the closet with the cordless phone from Finn's office, the only telephone around Heavenly Acres as far as she'd been able to determine.

She simply couldn't stand it anymore. It had been a whole week since she'd had a chance to talk to a real live woman, a friend, a confidante. If she didn't unburden herself soon, she was going to explode. Besides, she was worried.

Sitting on the floor of the closet, she pulled the door shut and ducked all the way into the back, behind the bottom of the fur coat. It was dark and strange in here, but quiet. And private.

Carefully, she punched in the number and sat back to wait until the line was picked up.

"Department of Housing Affairs," a voice rushed to tell her. "Can you hold?"

"Uh, yes," she started to say, but the voice was already gone and Muzak filled the line.

It seemed like ages before the harried switchboard operator came back. "Department of Housing Affairs," the woman blurted. "May I help you?"

"Extension 2247, please."

"Just a moment. I'll ring," she said, and then swooped back in to announce, "That line is busy. Will you hold?"

"Uh, yes. I'll hold."

Before she could catch her breath, the operator had raced away, and the Muzak was back. Angie didn't remember the department's phone service flying at this breakneck pace, but she supposed it was probably due to the on-going scandal and the ramifications of whatever Lance had pulled. It shouldn't be surprising they were getting so many phone calls.

Unfortunately, she kept having visions of her number being traced as she huddled there in the back of the closet. "Don't be ridiculous," she told herself. "Like they'd know it was me and start tracing by the way I said 'I'll hold.'"

The minutes ticked away, broken only by intermittent reminders from the switchboard that the extension she wanted was still busy. It seemed like she'd been there, in suspended animation, for hours. She hoped it was only minutes, or she was a sitting duck. And Finn was going to get one very expensive, very suspicious phone bill.

"I'd better be gone by the time the bill comes," she whispered. She'd worry about that later, when the time came. "It takes awhile for phone bills to come, doesn't it?"

There was no response from the fur coat, the only other occupant of the closet.

Finally, blessedly, the operator reported that she could put the call through. "Thank you," Angie offered, but the line was ringing, and her heart was beating like a tom-tom. She sat up straighter, silently begging Gretchen to answer her phone. One ring, two rings. Where was Gretchen?

"Public affairs liaison," a familiar voice said, and Angie almost blurted out who she was and where she was in her relief to hear the friendly voice.

But she held her tongue. In case Gretchen's phone was tapped, she'd decided on a strategy, and she launched it now, hoping her friend would figure out and play along. "Hello, Gretchen," she said slowly. "This is Bibi. Do you remember me?"

"Bibi?" the voice on the other end said doubtfully. "I don't think I know any..."

Angie's heart sank. *It's me,* she wanted to shout. But she kept her mouth shut and sent telepathic waves over the phone line.

"Oh, wait!" Gretchen exclaimed at the last moment. "Bibi! Of course. Sure, sure, I remember you. Bibi. Right. I haven't seen you in so long. Where are you?"

She poured on the fake cheer. "I'm not really sure. You know me—I end up wherever the wind blows me."

"Uh-huh. Wherever the wind blows you. Would that be an easterly wind, westerly, what?"

"Um, I don't know, actually." Safer for Gretchen not to know, even if she was understandably curious. Quickly, Angie changed the subject. "I'm really calling about *you*, Gretchen, not about me. I saw your name in the paper, about some big scandal. You are okay, aren't you?"

"Oh, I'm fine," Gretchen said brightly. "Actually, I'm better than fine. I was questioned, but I didn't really know anything, so that was over pretty fast. And you'll never believe it, but the FBI guy who got sent out to talk to me was just a doll, and he asked me out after the interview. We've been out twice now and I think I'm in love! Fun, huh?"

"Fun," Angie echoed weakly. Gretchen dating a fed? Maybe he was just trying to get close to her to pump her for information on her missing friend, the sex kitten. "Are you sure he's on the up-and-up?"

"Oh, yeah. Jake—that's his name, Jake Gannon—cute, huh? He's too honest to lie to me, if that's what you're thinking. And he also gave me the inside scoop on the investigation," Gretchen confided, lowering her voice. "He said they don't have any leads, so the woman that everyone is looking for could kind of relax a little, if I had any way of telling her that, which of course I don't. The last thing a fugitive like Angie Boone would do is contact me," she added loudly.

And that's when Angie knew for sure. Gretchen's phone was tapped.

"I'm just so glad to hear from you, I can't tell you," Gretchen went on. "Ever since you, uh, lost your job, I've been so worried." There was a long pause on the line, before Gretchen asked, "How are you, really? It isn't too bad out there in the cold, cruel world, is it?"

Even so far away, Angie could hear the concern in her friend's voice. It was wonderful to know that somebody—besides the police—cared what had happened to her.

"I got pretty lucky," she admitted. "I kind of fell into this place, sort of a shelter, where they don't ask any questions."

"Uh-huh. Well, that sounds interesting." Gretchen laughed. "I was wondering what you'd do for money. I imagined all kinds of exotic things."

Hearing Gretchen's laugh, Angie smiled. It was as if none of the bad things had happened. Her friend was still the same. And so was Angie. Except one of them was hiding in a closet a thousand miles from home. Angie felt more than a pang of misery as she crouched helplessly behind the fur coat.

"I miss you," she told Gretchen. "I've been feeling lately like I needed someone to talk to, and there just isn't anyone. Well, I guess there is someone, but I can't really confide in him. You understand."

Silence greeted her from Gretchen's end of the line. "Him? Are you telling me you met a guy?"

"Well, sort of. I mean, not in the way you think, but Gretchen..." Angie dropped her voice into its most confidential register. "He's gorgeous. Absolutely knock-your-socks-off, drop-dead gorgeous."

"So tell me about this guy. Is he nice? Does he have a job, is he married, can he type?"

A laugh bubbled out of her before she could hold it back. "I don't know," she said quickly. "I mean, he can be nice, when he wants to. And when he's acting really warm and cozy, I'm tempted to spill my guts and confess my sins and—"

"No, no, bad move," Gretchen interrupted. "In your situation, my dear, confession is the last thing you need. Can you, you know, string him along until things get sorted out?"

"If I knew how long that would take, maybe. But the problem is, if I wait till, um, *things* clear up," she said unhappily, "I won't be here to confide to anybody. I'll be home like a shot! I mean, this is a great place for a little R & R, but it's not my idea of a future."

"Oh," Gretchen said thoughtfully, "I get you. You have something a little more upscale in mind."

"Not just upscale. Uptown." She tried to piece it together not just for Gretchen, but for herself. It was getting difficult to remember who she was anymore, and maybe it would help to set it out, to remind herself. Angie shifted restlessly in her cramped position at the back of the closet. "Even if I can't put things back the way they were, at least I can get out of the boonies. There's nothing here for me."

"Nothing? What about the gorgeous guy?"

"Okay, there is him. But he hasn't exactly invited me to stay. Besides, I want to come home." Stubbornly, she said, "Right now, I'd sell my soul for a silk dress and a string of good pearls, a glass of wine with a plate of perfectly poached salmon, and for dessert, the biggest cup of coffee known to man."

"Coffee?"

"I can't have coffee here."

"Why not?"

"It's too complicated even to go into," she said with a laugh.

"So how long are you going to stay there, wherever it is you are?"

"As long as I can," she said softly. "Until somebody finds out and I have to move on, or it's all over and I can go back home."

"I don't know," Gretchen put it. "It sounds to me like you like it there pretty much, with this warm and cozy guy. I hate to say this, An—Bibi, but all that stuff about pearls and salmon, it was like you're trying to convince yourself. Is it possible you really don't want to leave the boonies, or this drop-dead hunk, even if your problems disappear tomorrow?"

"No," Angie said flatly. "Impossible."

"You're hedging, hon. I can hear it in your voice. You're hooked on this guy, aren't you?"

"He's not my type at all," she protested.

"When the temperature starts rising, type has nothing to do with it."

"It's about ten degrees outside at the moment."

"I'm not talking about outside," she said slyly.

"Look, I only called to make sure you were okay. I really shouldn't stay on the phone—"

"Okay, okay, have it your way." Gretchen added, "But thanks for calling, um, Bibi. I'm so glad to hear from you. Call again, soon? Let me know the next installment."

"There won't be another installment." Safe in her hiding place, Angie told herself what she'd really known all along—*there is no possibility of a future for me and Finn.*

She hated putting an end to this conversation, but she'd already tarried too long. "Bye, Gretchen...take care of yourself," she offered.

"You, too, hon. Be careful, okay?"

"Yeah. Careful."

Well, she was sure going to try.

Chapter Eight

Jake Gannon got so excited he almost spilled a full cup of coffee on his new wool pants. "I think I've got something!" he yelled at the only other person in the audio room, a middle-aged, balding federal agent named Al. "Hey, Al—the tapes from housing affairs, yesterday, from Gretchen Hearn's office—something just hit me."

Al barely lifted an eyebrow. "Whaddaya got?"

"It's mostly pretty normal, talking about guys and stuff..." He grinned sheepishly. "Gretchen mentioned me, said I was cute and a doll."

"Congratulations, lover boy," the other agent growled. "Is that it?"

"No, no, I mean, I think it's her—Angie Marie Boone—the other one on the line. Called herself Bambi or something, but just the way they were talking, it sounded like the right MO." He handed over the earphones. "Take a listen. See what you think."

After only a few moments, the second agent nodded gravely. "I think we got a live one, Jake. Pull the records at the phone company to see where she was calling from. Maybe we can get this Boone broad wrapped up right now."

As Al listened to the rest of the tape, scratching notes on a pad of paper, Jake dialed over to the records department at the telephone company's main office and fed in his security code. But he found out real quick it wasn't going to be that easy.

"Bad news," he told Al. "She called through the main switchboard at the DHA, and they transferred her upstairs to Gretchen's office. Their phones have been ringing off the wall for the last week, ever since this thing hit the fan." Jake's face was grim. "They're averaging about a thousand calls an hour, and people are getting put on hold for like twenty minutes waiting to be put through. The phone company records can tell us who called in the DHA switchboard, but not where or when they were transferred from there."

"So?" Al asked impatiently. "Do we have her or not?"

"Not." Jake shook his head. "All we know at this point is that Angie Marie Boone called in to the switchboard sometime yesterday morning, most likely between 10:30 and 11:30, since her call went through to Gretchen at 11:33. So we've got her number, all right, but we've got—" He referred to his notes. "—1,202 other people's numbers, too. And we don't know which one is hers."

"Aw, hell," Al rumbled. "Can't catch a break."

"You said it."

"All right, let's see what we got," he mused, ticking off the items on his list. "We'll run the whole she-bang, all one thousand whatever of them, through the computer, and eliminate anybody from the South or any place else it was warm yesterday. She said it was cold where she was."

"Right," Jake said eagerly, taking more notes.

"Plus, we can throw out any calls from cities or metro areas. The boonies, she said. Rural, or at least small town. If we come up with a match to a homeless shelter or a mission, so much the better."

Jake frowned. "It ain't much, but it's a start."

"Don't sweat it," his colleague said carelessly as he reviewed his notes from the phone conversation. "If we have to, we'll call every single one of those numbers ourselves. We'll get this Boone broad eventually."

"Yeah, well, we're not the only ones looking," Jake reminded him. "Let's just hope we get to her before the Goon Squad does."

"You said it." Al sighed heavily and ran a hand over his thinning hair. "Or there won't be a whole lot to find."

"FULL MOON," she whispered, gazing out her upstairs window into the pale, cold night.

Shivering from the chill coming off the window, she rubbed her arms and chided herself for standing there when a warm bed awaited. "But I'm not sleepy," she declared for the twentieth time. Just one more drawback to the slow-lane life-style at the farm, where there was absolutely nothing to do after all the kids had turned in for the night.

She wondered idly if Finn would be up for a game of checkers, even as she knew there was no way in the world she was going tripping down there in a T-shirt to ask him. Lighting for the moment on the end of the bed, Angie tucked her legs up under her and tried desperately to think of some way to occupy herself.

"I can worry some more," she said darkly. Ever since the furtive phone call to Gretchen, she'd been quaking in her boots that the number could've been traced and her location uncovered within seconds of placing the call. But if so, what were the authorities waiting for?

"Here I am. Come and get me," she muttered. Maybe a jail cell would be better than hanging around waiting for the ax to fall. Or for Finn to ensnare her in his web of perverse charm.

If you could tell me about it, I might be able to help. . . .

Finn's offer was very tempting, but one she was absolutely determined to resist.

"How could he help? What could he possibly do?"

The empty room provided no answers.

"Besides, he'd toss me out as soon as he found out," she told herself reasonably. "He'd have to, for the safety of the kids, no matter how many times he says he would try to help. It'd be straight off to jail without passing Go."

Except that that was a game, and Angie's life at the moment was no game. Allowing herself a small sigh, she slid back over to the window, to stare at the lonely moon, crossing her arms over Finn's T-shirt to ward away the chill.

Until she heard the noise.

Clomp, clomp, clomp, it went, breaking the heavy stillness of the night.

Immediately, Angie turned toward the sound. Downstairs. The kitchen maybe. What could it be?

The children should all be in bed by now, and they weren't allowed back in the main house after lights out. Besides, that awful stomping noise didn't sound like any child. More like Frankenstein's monster tromping on the floorboards.

She had a vague recollection of having heard a very similar sound before. But when? Why couldn't she remember?

Clomp, clomp. Louder and more insistent this time. *Clomp, Clomp, Clomp.*

And then it hit her. The first night. She'd been half asleep when a noise very like this one had awakened her.

"Another trick from Zero and his pals?" she speculated.

But what if it was an intruder, and Finn was fast asleep in the living room? What if the burglar was even at this moment leaning over Finn's sleeping form, ready to bash his head in with a club?

Or, even worse, what if the mob had found her? What if they were methodically searching the farm, bumping off whoever they fell over along the way?

Okay, so they were both pretty ludicrous scenarios. But what was that noise? And why hadn't Finn done anything to stop it?

Angie was coming unglued. If something bad was happening, and Finn was somehow incapacitated, it was up to her to defend the house. Grabbing the lamp off the bedside table, she slipped out of her room and tripped quietly down the stairs. Everything was dark and quiet, except for the occasional thump from the back of the house, reminding her that she wasn't crazy, that she really had heard something.

A draft shot up the bottom of her T-shirt, and she shivered, wishing she'd put on more clothes before she'd started this demented trek into the darkness. She certainly didn't see anyone, but she could still hear that damned noise. Stealthily, she made her way toward the back of the house, brandishing her lamp as she creaked open the door to the kitchen.

Before she had the door open more than an inch, it was wrenched out of her hand.

"Help," she cried, but a hand clamped down over her mouth.

As she kicked and struggled, a steely arm raked around her, dragging her all the way into the kitchen. The lamp she'd been holding crashed to the floor with enough noise to wake the dead, and the kitchen cat shot past her legs in a blur of fur.

Hauled into a viselike grip, she found herself half lying on the kitchen table, her T-shirt crumpled up somewhere around her belly button, the top half of her body plastered up against a warm, hard, completely bare chest.

"Angel," he said with disgust, pressing down harder and skewering her with his icy blue eyes. "I might have known."

She tried to wiggle out from under him, but that only made it worse, sliding her stomach over his, imprinting every single iota of his lean, hard body into her overheated skin.

"Heavens to Betsy," she whispered. It felt so good she almost forgot she was trapped on the kitchen table. She edged one leg out from under him, but it seemed to wrap around him, cradling him closer, without any conscious effort from her.

"Finn, please," she whispered, but she didn't know what she was begging for. All she knew was that she had an unbearable ache coming from the core of her being, and only he could ease the pain.

"What the hell do you think you're doing?" he growled.

"I don't know."

"You made me promise this wouldn't... Oh, the hell with it."

He released her then, swearing violently under his breath as he backed away from the table. Trying to catch her breath, Angie just lay there on the table, feeling as ripe and as ready as a Christmas goose.

"Get up, damn it," he said, sending her a ferocious scowl.

Taking her opportunity, Angie scrambled to a sitting position and pulled her T-shirt safely down over her thighs. As soon as she had a lap, the brown tabby jumped neatly into it. The cat sat there, eyeing her curiously as it delicately licked a paw.

Gingerly, she petted the small beast. "At least the cat likes me," she said under her breath.

She couldn't say the same for Finn. He was clearly furious, stalking back and forth in a disreputable pair of gym shorts that left less than nothing to the imagination. It might be dim in the kitchen, but not dark enough to hide Finn's spectacular attributes.

He had long, muscular legs, all sinew and strength, disappearing into his ragged shorts at a point that seemed ridiculous. Why bother with shorts when he was showing off that much thigh, that much... everything?

Angie groaned and tried to look away. But Finn's body kept drawing her gaze like a compass pointing north.

His beautiful, hard, smooth chest was bare, gleaming in the moonlight from the one small kitchen window. Angie tried not to lick her lips when she looked at his chest, but good gracious, the man was built. His shoulders were impossibly wide, his arms heavily muscled, more than she would've said she liked. Gazing at him, she decided she liked it just fine.

Whatever had been going on in the kitchen, Finn was in no way incapacitated. Scanning him now, angry and bare and magnificent, Angie could personally swear to the fact that he was fine.

"What in the hell did you think you were doing?" he demanded.

"I, uh..." Words failed her. She shook her head.

"I thought it was a prowler or something," he went on, in the same savage tone, slapping one fist into the other open palm. "But I suppose I should've known it would be you. Of all the idiotic, pea-brained stunts—traipsing around half dressed in the middle of the night—"

"Me?" she cried. "What about you? At least I'm *half* dressed. At least I have a shirt on!"

He just glared at her.

"Anyway, it wasn't my fault," she insisted. "I heard this awful noise, and it kept going on, so I thought you must be asleep, or knocked out or something—"

"Hold on just a second. Knocked out? Why would I be knocked out?"

Because the mob is after me? Well, she couldn't say that. "If the noise were a burglar," she explained coolly.

"And why do you suppose we'd have a burglar all the way out here, in the middle of nowhere, when we don't have anything to steal? How likely do you think that is?"

"Likely enough for you to ambush me in the kitchen and throw a running tackle on me," she retorted. "Or are you going to tell me you thought everything was on the up-and-up when you pinned me to the kitchen table?"

Once again, a murderous glare was Finn's answer.

"Gotcha," Angie said with satisfaction.

"I heard *you,*" he returned. "What do you expect me to think when I hear someone creeping around my house?"

Angie pulled down on the edge of her shirt, until she was sure she was covered as much as she was going to get covered. "We're even then, aren't we? You reacted the same way I did."

The kitten meowed loudly in her lap, and she scratched it behind the ears, until it spun over into a limp little ball.

"I was justified," he argued, "because *you* were up and sneaking around. But what's your excuse? What did you supposedly hear that made you so nervous?"

"A big, terrible, *clomping* noise," she said precisely. "I thought I'd better find out what it was, in case it was a burglar or something equally dangerous."

"So you came waltzing down here without any clothes on, carrying a lamp to scare away a burglar?"

"Well, it was the best I could do on short notice."

"And what exactly was this awful noise you heard?"

Now she had him. "These horrible footsteps, like Frankenstein, or maybe one of those zombies, you know, the ones who walk really slow with their arms straight out in front of them. Thump, thump, thump," she said slowly, going for effect. "Thump, thump, thump...like huge footsteps. I can't believe you didn't hear it."

"Frankenstein or a zombie, huh?"

As Angie looked on, mystified, Finn bent to pick up the cat's small bowl on the floor.

"I'm sure it's very kind of you to be so concerned with the cat's food supply," she said sweetly. "But what does this have to do with Frankenstein's footsteps?"

"It's not food, it's water," was his maddening reply, as he reached over and refilled the bowl from the tap, and then set it on the floor.

Immediately, the tabby perked up its ears and paid attention. Leaping crazily out of Angie's lap, it skidded over to the water bowl and took a few dainty sips, as if testing the water. Then the cat reached out a paw and bonked the heavy dish, sloshing water every which way and thumping the floor as the bowl tipped over and righted itself. The cat crouched low, twitching its hindquarters, making a game of shoving its water bowl around, under the table and back and forth across the floor, all the while creating the most abominable racket.

Angie could only stare.

"Frankenstein, I presume," Finn said lazily. "She does it all the time. It's one of her favorite tricks."

"It sounded terrible from upstairs," Angie said in her own defense.

"Uh-huh," he said, but his narrow lips were twitching.

"It really did! Don't you dare laugh at me, Finn. I was being brave, venturing down here in the dark. I thought you were hurt or something, and I was coming to the rescue. It's not my fault it was just ...''

The cat gave the bowl a vicious push just then, almost knocking the thing over completely, contributing a terrific splash and a boom to the conversation.

"Just a cat," Angie finished lamely.

"I guess you never had a cat," he ventured, "or you would've figured out the noise. Quite a few of them seem to play the same game with their bowls."

"Well, actually, we had lots of cats," she said absently. "But they lived out in the barn, to keep the mice down, not like real pets. After I was working and living by myself, I did think about getting a cat or a dog, to have some company, but then I was working so hard and hardly ever home, and it didn't seem fair. You know, fair to the—''

As she realized how much she'd said, Angie broke off abruptly, clamping a hand over her runaway mouth. The kitchen seemed very hot and stuffy all of a sudden, and Finn was awfully close. Angie's mouth went dry. What would he do with the information she'd carelessly given away? Would it be the key to uncovering her identity, discovering her dirty secrets?

"Don't sweat it," he interjected. "God, Angel, from the look on your face, you'd think you just confessed to the Great Train Robbery." He shook his head. "Let me tell you, Angel, what you said is nothing I didn't already know. I figured out you grew up on a farm a long time ago, and since you sure weren't happy about being back on one, it didn't take a genius to guess that you left as soon as you were old enough, aiming for a big career in the city. I mean, I have eyes and ears, Angel. So I added a few things up."

"Good for you," she whispered.

He wiped wet hands down the front of his shorts, edging the waistband down just enough to graze the top of his hard hips. Angie bit down on her lip, reminding herself to keep breathing.

Hellfire. The last thing she needed to do was to share confidences with this man in this suffocating kitchen, to see his fabulous body paraded around in front of her in all its glory. Her nipples stiffened under the soft T-shirt, and she quickly crossed her arms over her chest. What would she do next to betray herself?

"No harm, no foul," he said, narrowing his gaze at her.

Checking out his minuscule shorts with the briefest of glances, she was crying foul, even if he wasn't. "Look," she broke in nervously, climbing off the table and making for the door, with her arms still securely crossed over her front, "I have to get out of here."

"Angel, listen." He moved in closer, reaching out a hand to her as she backed up uneasily. "It doesn't matter if you drop hints around me, okay? I've told you before, you're safe with me. I won't judge you, and I won't think you're an awful person. I'm on your side."

So he was on his problem-solving kick again. That old damsel-in-distress stuff she found so annoying.

"Uh-huh, right. Well, if that's all . . ."

"Yeah, okay," he said reluctantly. "Now that we both know nobody's in any danger from the cat, I guess we might as well call it a night."

"Right," she returned, skirting around him and his biceps as she made for the hallway and the stairs.

As she navigated the first step, she winced. Lucky her; she was the proud owner of a brand new bruise on one hip. It wasn't tough to figure out where that came from. Recalling her perilous position underneath Finn on the kitchen table, she decided she ought to be grateful just to be up and around in one piece.

But she couldn't help wondering what he would've done if she'd hung on when he'd pinned her down underneath him, how he would've reacted if she'd wound her arms around his neck and slid her fingers over those shoulders, refusing to let go. What if she'd said, "Make love to me, Finn. Right now, right here"?

Maybe if she'd kissed him, good and hard, he would've let up on the inquisition. He would've had to. If his mouth was otherwise occupied, he couldn't very well ask questions, could he?

In that direction lies madness, she told herself. *So stop thinking about his mouth, already.*

But, with her hand on the railing, she hesitated. She could see him already settling into his makeshift bed on the sofa, as she called down into the murky living room. "Finn?"

"Yeah?"

She knew she was skating on thin ice, but she couldn't help herself. "I thought maybe you would apologize for tackling me like that, on the kitchen table."

"Why would I apologize?" He rolled over inside his sheet, and his words were muffled as his head dipped into the pillow. "I'm not the least bit sorry."

Neither am I, she thought fervently. *Neither am I.*

JoJo "THE MONGOOSE" Mando was a happy man. The boss had sent him on an errand, and he had good news. Well, sorta good news. Coulda been better, but hey, it was information, and that's why the boss paid him the big bucks.

Information and intimidation. Those were JoJo "the Mongoose" Mando's specialties. JoJo smiled, rearranging his too-tight tie, shifting his shoulders inside his forty-six-short jacket. Information and intimidation. Who could ask for more?

"Hey dere, Mr. Anthony," he said respectfully, wedging his barrel-chested body through the narrow doorway into the boss's specially-made steam room. "I am happy to report to you that I have acquired the information we discussed, regarding one missing broad from the Department of Affairs and Houses."

"Housing Affairs, JoJo," grunted Lou "Elevator Man" Anthony. "Close the door, will ya?"

Mr. Anthony was called "Elevator Man" as a result of his early predilection for using empty elevator shafts as a method of disposing of those with whom he had professional disagreements. Now that he was older and more upscale, he had abandoned elevators and adopted JoJo as his enforcer.

"You're smiling, JoJo," the Elevator Man remarked, hitching up the towel knotted around his waist. "It ain't easy to tell, but I always know, when your neck disappears, you got good news for me. So tell me, JoJo, you found the lady, huh? We got my money in the palm of our hand, yes?"

JoJo shook his head. He rolled a beefy hand across his forehead to catch the sweat rivulets pouring down his florid face. "Sorry, Mr. A. I got no lady." The sweat continued to pour. "But I do got a lead."

"A lead?" Anthony struggled to his feet, almost losing his grip on his towel. "Where's the broad, JoJo? She's been gone a week, and I got a million bucks that went up in smoke with her. I ain't a patient man, JoJo."

"Yeah, yeah, I know exactly what you mean, Mr. Anthony," JoJo hastened to assure his boss. "But, listen, what I got is this, see—the broad called her pal at Houses and Affairs. The feds got the place wired and we got the feds wired, so, presto, we got what they got. Right now, they got a big list of phone numbers, and they're pushing pencils to figure out which one belongs to the right broad. I figure, we get the list, we send some muscle out, it's a lot faster than the feds playing nice-nice, right?"

"I don't pay you to think, JoJo," the Elevator Man said ominously. "Get me the list. On the double." He frowned, pulling his eyes even closer together under thick, fierce brows. "I want that broad."

"Yes, Mr. Anthony," JoJo rumbled, hurrying to back out of the steam room before he melted.

Feeling a whole lot cooler and a whole lot cockier, JoJo smiled as he strolled out into the opulent hallway of the boss's town house. *Find the broad.* In other words, use information and intimidation. JoJo "the Mongoose" Mando's specialties.

HE COULD HEAR HER up there again tonight.

It was getting to be a marathon of insomnia. Upstairs in his room, Angel roamed back and forth from the bed to the window, from the window to the bed, the floorboards above him groaning anxiously to herald her journey.

He could feel her restlessness, jagged and uneasy, as if it were his own. Hell, it was his own.

In his lonely, lumpy bed, Finn twisted around to a sitting position. He rubbed his head between his hands, irritated at his own inability to sleep. What the hell was wrong with her, anyway? Why did she have to keep pacing up there, like a caged animal at the zoo?

Because she's as wound up as you are, and for the same damn reason.

Funny, he hadn't noticed how much he swore until Angel pointed it out. Or maybe he hadn't sworn so much until Angel started driving him crazy.

Whatever the sequence of events, he couldn't stand another night like this. First it had been the cat and the water bowl, then last night Angel had slipped through the living room on the pretext that she'd left her shoes downstairs and didn't want anyone tripping over them in the morning.

As he played her waiting game, he wondered what her excuse would be tonight. Because she would come up with one. It was only a matter of time before she came drifting down the stairs and into the living room, a ghostly night vision, sliding nervous hands over the back of the chair, gazing at him as he pretended to be safely asleep, mouthing his name in the softest of voices until he couldn't take it anymore.

He was trying desperately to hold on to his principles, to hang on to his plan for a solitary, selfless life spent in the service of others. That kind of life couldn't include hanky-panky with a woman hiding as many secrets as this one—it was as simple as that. But it sure wasn't easy in the face of this kind of assault.

Above him, Angel's floorboards echoed her every footstep, and Finn felt the reverberations deep in his soul. With one violent movement, he threw himself facedown on the couch and slammed the pillow over his head.

No more creaky floors. Silence.

"Aw, hell," he grumbled, sitting back up. He heaved the pillow at the rocking chair across the room, setting the rocker swaying in the stillness. He now knew it was even worse not to hear, to lie there imagining what she was doing. At least with sound effects, he could be sure. And he could prepare himself for her trek downstairs into his arena, step by step, as she descended the stairs.

His lips curved into a nasty smile. Maybe he ought to lay a trap tonight, stick something gruesome in his bedclothes on the couch and let her discover it. Maybe that would cure his wandering Angel of her late-night visits. Or he could vacate the place entirely—go bunk out with the boys or something—and let Angel torture an empty living room. Although that was hardly a solution.

No, the best idea seemed to be to have it out, to wait till she invaded his turf one more time, and then blister her pretty behind.

Finn crossed his arms behind his head and lay back against the armrest. His smile widened. "We'll just see who tortures whom, Angel," he muttered under his breath. "You come down here tonight and I won't be responsible for the consequences."

He didn't have long to wait. Only moments after he'd decided he was going to enjoy round three of the Battle of the Bedrooms, Angel's footfalls trod lightly down the stairs.

"Finn?" she called softly from the landing. "Are you awake?"

He refused to answer. Instead, he closed his eyes, turned as far as he could into the blankets and concentrated on steady, rhythmic breathing.

"Are you asleep?" she asked quietly, tiptoeing over nearer the couch and peeking into its depths.

Finn stayed mute, taking nice, even breaths. He thought of adding a light snore, but rejected the notion, afraid of gilding the lily. Instead, he focused on rhythm. Inhale, exhale. As his chest rose and fell, he took a perverse kind of joy in his little charade. Unless he was totally off the mark, Angel would be exasperated and peeved to find him deep in an untroubled sleep.

"Finn?"

As she leaned in from the front of the sofa, he couldn't help but inhale the faint scent of flowers that clung to her hair, wafting out over him as she brushed him with the trailing tendrils.

Damn her and her sweet smell. It was hard not to lose his patience and go for it right then, but Finn continued the subterfuge. Inhale, exhale. Let her hover over him, like an avenging angel. Let her damn hair flicker over his wrist, and her soft, sexy voice repeat his name until he was out of his mind.

Hell, he was already out of his mind.

When she was as close as she could be, edging the couch, he took his chance. Without warning, he lunged. Before she knew what hit her, he'd grabbed her and pulled her underneath him. He sat there on his haunches, feeling very sure of himself after hours of tension and uncertainty. *King of the hill,* he thought.

With her slim hips trapped between his knees, Finn grinned down at her.

"You play with fire, Angel, you're going to get burned."

And then he bent all the way down, cradled her face in his hands, and kissed her.

Chapter Nine

His mouth was hard and brazen, wet and arrogant, as it slashed across hers, asking nothing, demanding everything.

She'd never been kissed like this, with such intensity, such single-minded desperation, as if his life depended on branding her with his mouth.

She couldn't breathe, couldn't think, and it didn't matter. Dazed, seething, she pressed her mouth into his, harder, deeper, wrapping her arms around his neck and hanging on tight. All she wanted was more of him, more of his mouth, more of this hot, slick seduction.

If he'd told her then to take off all her clothes, she would have. If he'd demanded she become his love slave, she would've said "yes" without a moment's hesitation.

Thank goodness he couldn't keep up the kiss forever, or she might have been lost.

When he finally had to break away to breathe, leaving her supine in the depths of the couch, Angie could only lie there, eyes wide open, dizzy and confused. Tiny stars twinkled in her periphery. She felt thoroughly kissed, and thoroughly depraved. Limply, she dropped a hand over her forehead, like some Victorian maiden with a case of the vapors.

Lord save me, I just kissed this man like there was no tomorrow. I just kissed this man with everything I had, and it wasn't enough. I wanted him; I still want him.

"I am a sick, sick person," she whispered.

Finn said nothing, just sat back on his haunches and looked pleased with himself.

"You weren't asleep at all," she said between gritted teeth. She struggled to knock him off balance and off the couch, but he held his ground on top of her. "Scared the life out of me."

As she wiggled under him, he said darkly, "Feels to me like you got plenty of life left in that body."

Angie stilled her struggle. "Okay, I give up. You win," she said in a small voice. "You fooled me, you kissed me, you had your fun. So you win, okay?"

"I'm not the one who's playing games."

He bent down very close to her face, taking her on eye-to-eye, making her think he might kiss her again. Could she stand it if he did? Could she stand it if he didn't?

He didn't. He just tantalized her for a long moment and then edged away to the end of the couch. Dragging herself up to a sitting position, she told herself she was safe from him and his dangerous embrace for the moment. So why did she feel like hitting something? Or someone? Preferably him.

"You're the one who keeps dancing down here, trying to stir up trouble," he went on, in the same cynical, husky voice. "Well, Angel, looks like you got trouble. Now what?"

"I wasn't trying to stir up trouble," she said weakly. "It was just...I couldn't sleep. I thought maybe you would talk to me."

"Talk wasn't what you had in mind."

"Wh-what do you mean?"

From his end of the sofa, he shot her a reckless smile. "You've been trying to seduce me for three nights now."

"That's crazy," she returned immediately, but she knew it was a feeble protest at best. "You're the one who's all over me. I was standing there, minding my own business, when you ambushed me again. And this is after you promised that there wouldn't be any...funny business between us. You promised!"

"Yeah, but you promised, too. But then you decided to torture me every night, parading around and poking at me, not letting me sleep."

"I wasn't trying to...Oh, forget it." She rose from the couch, feeling like an absolute idiot. "You made your point. I'll go back to bed now. I promise not to torture, parade or poke anymore, okay?"

"No," he said harshly, catching at her arm as she tried to walk past him. He yanked her back down next to him, to their battlefield on the sofa. "You promised before. I don't think you'll keep it this time, either."

"Look, I'm sorry."

She turned her gaze directly on him, trying to appeal to his better instincts with wide, imploring eyes. She knew he had a soft side; she'd seen him use it with the children. Where was Finn's tenderness when she needed it?

"Sorry isn't good enough."

"What is?"

His lips pressed into a hard line. "I don't know."

"Do you want me to leave?" she asked in a low, uneven voice. "Is that it? Go away forever?"

"No," he shot back. "That's not what I want."

Angie shivered, and she rubbed her arms, pretending she was cold in the drafty living room. Sitting this close to Finn, she was roasting. "So why are you acting like this, if me leaving isn't the solution?"

The answer came like a shot. "Because I'm sick and tired of this, that's why," he snapped. "I can't take this cat-and-mouse stuff anymore."

"Me, either," she whispered. She sent him a caressing gaze. "Me, either."

He stood up abruptly, stalking back and forth in front of the couch, slashing a hand through his hair. "I can't sleep knowing you're up there, in *my* bed, half covered in *my* clothes. I can't eat, I can't think— my temper is rotten, so I'm a jerk to the kids—all because I know night is going to come and you'll be haunting me again."

"Haunting you?" She'd never thought of herself that way, as a sexy siren, preying upon a man's thoughts, obsessing his sleeping and waking hours.

"Don't think I'm fooled," he said bitterly. "I know what you've been doing—hoping I'd reach the end of the line—that I'd grab you and make love to you and then it would be my fault, not yours.''

His restless journey brought him to a stop near the front window. Outside, the Heavenly Acres sign, painted with its own more innocent angel, pitched and lurched in the unforgiving winter wind. As Finn stood there, silent, gazing out into the night, Angie was struck again by the cold elegance of his profile.

She wanted so badly to touch him, to take away the sadness and the frustration, but she knew she couldn't begin to help him. But maybe she could help herself.

"Finn?" He didn't turn. It was better that way. What she had to say might be more easily done if she didn't have to look him in the eye. "Maybe we should stop denying whatever it is that's happening between us."

"Denying?"

"It seems pretty obvious we're both feeling the same sorts of—" Angie wetted her lips. "—disturbing thoughts."

He hitched a look at her from beneath half-lowered lids. "What disturbs you, Angel?"

"I can't sleep," she said simply. "I can't sleep because I can't stop thinking about you, Finn, down here in the moonlight. I know what you wear to sleep in," she whispered, "and what you don't wear."

Across the room, Finn went very still.

Slowly, carefully, Angie continued. "I feel so drawn to come down here, as if I were . . . hypnotized. Something about you, or about us, is forcing me to walk down those stairs and venture over the line, to push the limits, to drive into the deep water. What is it? What's happening, Finn?"

"We both know," he muttered. "Don't we?"

"Do we? Or is it just that we're the only adults around for miles? I mean, two people thrown together, the *Blue Lagoon* syndrome, you know."

"No," he said clearly. "That's not it."

"I didn't think so, either," she said softly. "And not just because I'm a damsel in distress, either. When you look at me, you see me and not my troubles."

"I can't deny that."

"Good. So we agree that we've developed this unquenchable..." Angie swallowed past a suddenly dry throat. "Lust." There, she'd said it. "We've developed an unquenchable lust for each other. So maybe what we should do is..." Picking her way through verbal land mines, she finished up in a rush. "Maybe the best thing for both of us would be to just get it over with."

He spun around to stare at her, and his mouth fell open as she watched. And then he began to laugh—loud, hard guffaws that shattered the stillness in the room.

"I can't believe you're hooting like that," she said stiffly.

"Oh, Angel, you're priceless," he said when he collected himself enough to talk. "You sit there with all that hair, tangled and messed up every which way, wearing a T-shirt that hides absolutely nothing, with lips that have obviously just been kissed—and kissed good—and you know what you look like? You look like the Playmate of the Month, Angel, only better—

hotter, softer, sexier—like a woman every man in the world would want to take to bed.''

Angie felt her cheeks suffuse with warmth. She held her tongue to hide her acute embarrassment. The Playmate of the Month? Was that what she was reduced to?

''And then,'' he went on, ''you open that sweet, soft little mouth of yours, and you come right out and hit me with a proposition. Yeah, that's right—you suggest we should sleep together, have ourselves a hot night or two, but you say it in this prissy way that sounds like a *National Geographic* field trip. Want to go collect feldspar in the outer Yucatán? Or maybe you'd rather *get it over with* and make love to me? Yeah, right.''

She rose from the sofa with all the dignity she could muster, which was difficult wearing a T-shirt accused of hiding absolutely nothing. ''Obviously, this was a bad idea and we should end this discussion right now.''

''I have one more thing to say, Angel.''

She looked up. ''Well?''

''If and when we make love, it won't be to get it over with.'' He gazed out into the cold winter's night, and his features looked surprisingly vulnerable, surprisingly soft. ''It will be because we both want to, because we care about each other and trust each other. That's the only way I want to make love with you—no secrets, no holds barred. Got it?''

''Oh, yeah, I've got it,'' she mumbled. She moved quickly to the stairs. She might be willing to lend him her body for a while, but she had never intended to give away her soul. *No holds barred.* She shivered. That wasn't at all what she'd intended.

She took the first three steps up before his voice stopped her.

"Oh, and Angel?" he asked.

She didn't turn. "What?"

"See that you get something else to sleep in, will you? Wearing my T-shirt to bed is very dangerous."

SINCE HER SLEEP had been fitful at best, she couldn't have said how or when he managed it. But when she woke in the morning, she found a voluminous white nightgown and a heavy robe draped over the foot of her bed.

"I guess it was important to him," she muttered. Her hands shook as she stripped off his damn T-shirt and threw it into the farthest corner of the room.

Trust Finn Sheridan to find a store open in the middle of the night. Trust him to buy her a beautiful cotton nightgown with exquisite lace at the neck, and a thick, lush, terry-cloth robe with an insignia on the pocket—exactly what she would've picked out for herself if given the chance. Trust him to make both of them four sizes too big.

Trust Finn Sheridan to tick her off so completely she couldn't see straight.

"I despise that man," she told herself fiercely.

So why did she already miss the smell and the feel of his T-shirt?

"ANGEL, ANGEL," the small boy said excitedly. He ran into the playroom at full speed and started tugging on her sleeve. "I saw baby foxes out behind the haystack. They're in this little hole. Will you come look, please, please, please?"

Derek had used three complete sentences, and pronounced all the words right, including *fox*, when he always seemed to have trouble with *x*. He was already doing so much better, and Angie felt she deserved a lot of the credit. See how far a little special attention could go?

Angie beamed at Derek as she scooped him up for a hug. "Baby foxes, huh? Sounds great. But it'll have to wait until I can borrow a coat from Finn."

The weather had taken a turn for the colder yesterday, and running around outside with no coat, or only a thin one, just wouldn't cut it. Trotting out a fox fur to check on baby foxes seemed the epitome of bad taste.

"But Finn gone," Derek complained. "How long before the foxes?"

"Finn *is* gone," she corrected him, ruffling his hair. "And please don't whine. I don't know how long he'll be gone. Where did he go, do you know?"

"P'lice station," Derek said with a good deal of importance.

"The police? Are you sure?" She'd asked the question because she was glad, relieved, *thrilled* Finn wasn't hanging around making her want to murder him, as usual. But she hadn't planned on hearing he'd gone off to talk to the authorities, for goodness' sake! "Why would he go to the police?"

"Dunno." Derek shrugged his narrow shoulders. "Maybe a new kid."

"You mean, maybe the police are turning a new child over to Finn? Like someone from the street, maybe?"

"Uh-huh," Derek said cheerfully. "Or maybe somebody from here's in trouble, like stole suthing. It happened before once."

"Somebody stole something and the police were involved?"

"Uh-huh. A big boy stole a car. Boy, was Finn mad!" Derek's brown eyes grew large and round. "He yelled and yelled. I never seen Finn so mad!"

"I never *saw*," Angie supplied absently. If Finn was mad about car theft, what would he think about the politico's sex kitten? Of course, she hadn't really done anything wrong, and she certainly wasn't anybody's sex kitten, but there was no reason to suppose he or anyone else would believe her. "Let's hope it's just another new child, and not trouble." *And let's hope it has nothing to do with me.*

"Yeah. But it was kinda funny when Finn was so mad." Derek giggled as he found a race car on the floor to play with. "Vroom, vroom," he hollered. He smiled innocently up at Angie. "Maybe Finn will be real mad and yell again."

"Sooner or later, he probably will," she said gloomily.

"Umm, Angel?"

Angie turned in time to see Layla shuffling her feet impatiently in the doorway to the small playroom. "Hi, Layla. Derek and I are going out later to see a nest of baby foxes. Want to come?"

"No way," she scoffed. "That's really dumb."

Derek hurled his car at her. "Not dumb."

"Totally and *bogusly* dumb," Layla retorted, whipping the car back at her brother.

"Stop it!" Angie commanded, stepping in between before either of them could escalate the warfare. She also confiscated the car to prevent another round trip. "Layla, did you want something?"

Layla rolled her eyes, but refrained from making further snide comments. "I wanted to talk to you, *alone,*" she stressed. "So scram, Derek, okay?"

"I guess that would be all right." Angie picked up a pile of cars and poured them into Derek's pockets. "Why don't you take these and run them around the tables in the woodworking room? I don't think anyone is using it right now."

Derek looked doubtful, but he took off with the cars, stopping outside the door to screech, "Layla is a dogface!" before running on his way.

"He is such a baby," his sister said darkly.

"Well, he's getting better," Angie tried.

As an older sister herself, she knew it would be years before these two stopped harassing each other. Her brothers hadn't even gotten warmed up till their teenage years.

She gazed at Layla with new sympathy. "What can I do for you, Layla? You said you wanted to talk to me?"

"Uh-huh." Layla skirted around, finally lighting on a small plastic chair underneath a poster.

"So what's up?"

"Well..." Layla twisted a long strand of hair around her finger and started kicking at the carpet.

"Well?"

"Well..."

"Layla, please, can we get to the point?"

"Well..." The girl glanced up suddenly, her eyes curious and bright under an untidy fringe of bangs. "Woman to woman..."

Uh-oh. With that kind of opening, Angie knew she was in trouble.

"I need to know about sex."

Angie winced. As she wondered what in the world she was going to say, Layla just sat there, staring, chewing on her hair from time to time, completely unconcerned that she'd thrown Angie onto the horns of a moral dilemma.

Uncomfortable silence hung between them for several moments until Angie asked, "What exactly are we talking about here?"

"Sex," Layla repeated. "You know."

"Like the birds and the bees?"

"Huh?"

"Like where babies come from?"

"No," Layla said impatiently. *"S-E-X."*

"I know how to spell it," Angie returned. "I just don't know what to tell you."

"What a drag." Layla's mouth turned down at the corners. "I guess if you don't know, like, you don't know. Except, aren't you kind of *ancient* to be a virgin?"

"Wait just a second—"

"Am I interrupting something?" Finn asked languidly, bracing his large body against the small door to the children's playroom.

"Yes!" Angie hissed as Layla jumped to her feet.

"Finn, Finn, I'm so glad you're here!" the little traitor called out. "I want to know about sex. I asked Angel, but she's a virgin so she doesn't know. So do you know, Finn?"

"I didn't say I didn't know," Angie muttered.

"Well, Layla, let's talk about it, okay?" Unfazed by the subject matter, Finn chatted quietly with the young girl for several minutes, as Angie sat on her side of the room, feeling like a real bozo. Why was it so easy for him and so tough for her?

Finally, with her curiosity apparently satisfied, Layla set off to look at a book Finn recommended, and he turned to Angie. All he did was arch an eyebrow, and she began to steam.

"Don't start with me," she said, raising a warning hand. "I never said I knew what to tell a kid about that kind of thing. Not that I think she should even know about that, mind you. I mean, *eleven* is a bit young, don't you think, to be talking about—"

"Chill out, will you?" He stood there, looking big and scary as he loomed over the tiny children's toys scattered around the room. "Turns out one of the other girls told her you can get cooties from kissing a boy, and she wanted to know if it was true."

"Well, she said sex, not cooties or kissing." As a matter of fact, she had repeated the word "sex" about fourteen times.

He shrugged. "She doesn't know the semantics."

"I could've told her she wouldn't get cooties," Angie groused. "Don't stand there thinking you're so smart."

Finn shook his head, but there was a gleam of mischief in his brilliant blue eyes. "So, you're a virgin, huh?"

Angie took a deep breath and tried not to kill him. Perhaps the best option would be to leave the room quietly before she was completely humiliated.

"Maybe you thought I didn't catch it when Layla dropped that little bomb," he said mockingly. "Are you a virgin, Angel?"

"I don't think it's any of your business what I am," she said sweetly.

"That would explain the 'getting it over with' thing. I mean, if you've never done it before, you might want to get it out of the way. Makes sense to me."

He was severely trying her patience. "That's not what I meant, and you know it."

"So you aren't a virgin, then?"

Under her breath, she muttered, "Sometimes you're really insufferable, you know that?"

"Insufferable?" he asked lazily. "You didn't think so last night."

"And you have the maturity level of a four-year-old."

"I'm just teasing you, Angel," he offered in his own defense. "Come on, it was funny. If you'd seen the look on your face when Layla said, 'Aren't you kind of *ancient* to be a virgin?' It was hysterical."

"I don't think it's so funny."

He just stood there, grinning at her, until Angie had the irresistible urge to wipe that smug look off his face once and for all. Reaching behind her, she picked up a big pillow off the floor. It was large and square, with "Sesame Street" characters printed on it.

Reeling back, she slugged him with it, as hard as she could, right across the chest. And then she laughed out loud.

He stuck up his arms as a half-hearted defense, alternately shielding his body and trying to get the pillow away from Angie. "So *I'm* the one with the maturity of a four-year-old?" he asked sarcastically.

"You provoked me."

And she belted him another one. It felt great, better than anything had in a long time. As Finn backed up, she kept punching him with the cushion, following up a satisfying smash to his hard abdomen with an off-balance whack on the hip.

"This one's for making fun of me. And this one's for treating me like a child. And this one..." She took a big windup. "This one is for ridiculing me about that execrable virgin thing."

As she struck again, he spun around and caught her in a bear hug from behind, pinning her arms to her sides. Her pillow dangled from her fingertips, useless. All she could do was struggle against the iron bonds of his arms, but she wasn't getting very far.

"Stop it," he ordered, pointedly removing her weapon from her grasp. "This is really silly. But I don't believe in violence, not even with a pillow."

"Fine," she said evenly, as he finally released her. He might be able to overpower her, but he couldn't take away the licks she'd gotten in. And smacking him with the cushion had felt *so* good.

He threw himself onto a child-size beanbag chair, making a ludicrous picture of a big, rangy man overpowering a poor, defenseless chair. "So what's your problem?" he demanded, sitting up enough to brace the pillow on his knees.

Angie decided she preferred to stand. She gave him a saucy smile. "Actually, I feel much better now."

"Great," he said acidly. "I don't." Without warning, he reached out and slammed the foam pillow against a nearby plastic chair, toppling it with one vicious crunch.

Angie tried not to flinch. "Feel better now?"

"No, as a matter of fact, I don't."

She shook her head, letting long, curly wisps drift across her face. "You sure seem to be storing up a lot of stress. That's not healthy, you know," she commented sweetly, very sure her words would make him crazy. She didn't know why she derived such satisfaction from antagonizing him, but it always seemed to work out that way. "Maybe you ought to find an outlet for all that tension."

He glanced up, his blue eyes enigmatic. "Is this leading to something? Like maybe you're thinking of offering to 'get it over with' again?"

"Not in this lifetime," she said with spirit. "No, out of the goodness of my heart, I was thinking more of telling you to get out, enjoy yourself, go into town, seek adult companionship."

"I go into town once a week."

"Yeah, to get groceries." She pooh-poohed that with a wave of her hand. "In case nobody ever told you, there's more to life than groceries."

"So, Mother Teresa, you're thinking I should go to a bar, pick up a good-hearted woman, blow off a little steam?"

It was exactly what she'd been proposing, but it sounded hideous when she heard it straight out like that. Her thoughts suddenly sent her a picture of Finn drinking in some tacky tavern, one booted foot propped on the bar rail. In her mind's eye, a sloshed, sleazy woman sidled up, rubbing her disgusting body against Finn. And then this imaginary piece of cheap trash leaned in over Finn's arm, parading her overflowing breasts in front of his eyes. Yechh. The notion was horrifying.

"Well, maybe you should forget the good-hearted woman. There is disease control to consider."

"Does that include you?"

"Me?" She was mystified. How did she fit into the picture of the trashy bar? "What about me?"

"Well," he said, leaning back in the beanbag chair, stretching out his long, blue-jeaned legs. "I thought maybe you were asking me out on a date."

Chapter Ten

"A date?" The idea of a date with Finn Sheridan was too silly to even contemplate.

"Yeah." His narrow lips curved into a knowing smile. "Now that you've given up on throwing your body at me to relieve the tension, I thought maybe you were throwing your mind at me, like keeping me occupied for a night out."

"Well, I might... I mean, if the circumstances were right." Angie chewed her lip. "A date?"

"Are you asking?"

"As my civic duty, maybe I could do that," she said lightly. Even as she said it, she knew what a date between them would be reduced to. Five minutes into it, they'd either be panting with lust or fighting to the death. But she couldn't seem to stop herself. "Maybe that would be a good idea. Just to make sure you don't blow up and die of a heart attack, from keeping all that hostility inside."

"Well, sorry, but I don't need a social worker," he told her. "Thanks for asking and everything, but I don't take it too kindly when people offer to do things for me for my own good.''

''I didn't ask!''

''I can't go, anyway.'' He shoved himself up out of the beanbag. ''I don't do 'dates.' Nobody to look after this place if I do.''

''Are you telling me you never go out on dates?''

''Isn't that what I just said?''

''Holy smokes. You're in worse shape than I thought.'' Angie stared at him. ''Finn, this is serious. Everybody needs recreation, a little time away from responsibility.''

''Aw, come on, Angel.'' He shrugged. ''You know as well as I do. I can't afford a night away.''

''So if you can't afford a night away, I suppose that means you never take a vacation, never let someone else handle the headaches for a while?''

''No,'' he said calmly. ''So what?''

''What about Floyd? Couldn't he handle it?''

''Floyd?'' Finn laughed. ''If I left him in charge, they'd eat him alive.''

''Oh, come on. Floyd can handle them just fine. You just like to think you're irreplaceable, that's all.'' Stubbornly, she maintained, ''It's not healthy. All work and no play...''

He shrugged those wonderful shoulders. ''I do what I want to do.''

''And what you want to do is bury yourself out here like some monk, with no social life, no *nothing?* Are you crazy?''

She could tell he was starting to get a bit defensive. She could see it in the line of his jaw.

"My life is just fine, Angel. Maybe you better look out for your own."

"But, Finn," she persisted, "you only have half a life. I mean, don't get me wrong, the kids are great. What you sacrifice for the kids is great. But you have to have more in your life than that. What is there for *you,* for Finn?"

His eyes grew cold. "Look, I have a good idea what your values are. I figure you as aiming to be the youngest manager ever in the history of the XYZ Corporation, or maybe the first female partner at the firm, whatever—it doesn't matter." His mouth curved into a mocking line. "All those selfish, materialistic, yuppie goals are the same."

"There's nothing wrong with wanting to accomplish something."

"Not at all." He gave her a speculative glance. "But getting a fancier house or a more impressive title on your office door isn't much of an accomplishment in my book."

"So wasting your life on a bunch of juvenile delinquents who'll never appreciate it, anyway, is the be-all and end-all, huh?"

"They're not juvenile delinquents," he said curtly. "They're just kids. And they need me."

Angie wished she had the pillow back long enough to knock the chip off his shoulder. "What in the world did you do, back when you ran away, that you're still paying penance?"

"Penance?" he asked. "What the hell does that mean?"

"You—here," she said, gesturing with one hand. "St. Finn the Altruistic."

"I don't know what that means, either," he said coolly.

"Oh, you do, too." Angie crossed her arms over her chest and glared at him. "You're one of the smartest men I ever met, and I can tell you know exactly what I'm saying. You just pretend not to understand because it fits your image better."

"I don't have an image."

"You do, too. You're crawling with it." After hanging around with politicians for the better part of five years, Angie understood image. "The way you stand, the way you talk, the way you curl up your lip and get all steely-eyed when people stand up to you—it's all part of this chip-on-your-shoulder business."

"You lost me, sweetheart," he said sardonically. "Penance and chips, curly lips—I don't get any of it."

"Oh, right," she shot back. "You only understand plain talk, right? Maybe this will be simple enough for you—you're hiding here on this farm because you think you screwed up in the real world."

"I'm not hiding anywhere," he argued. "You have a corner on that market."

"You're hiding," Angie insisted. She was still trying to think this through. "Okay, so you were a bad boy. So now you're sacrificing your life to make up for whatever it was you did wrong when you were a kid. Or maybe it's what your parents did wrong." She saw the scowl on his face and she knew she'd hit pay dirt. "Maybe your ritzy parents weren't very nice people, and you think you're taking a stand by refusing their money."

"Holy hell," he swore. "My parents are off limits. What do you know about them, anyway?"

On a roll, she simply ignored his interruptions and kept right up with her quickie psychological analysis. "You know, Finn, the only one who's paying the price is *you*. You can take in six new runaways every day, you can feed them and keep them and send them back out into the world. But you'll still be all alone when it's over—just you and that Heavenly Acres sign flapping in the breeze."

"And what about you?"

That stopped her in her tracks. "What about me?"

"You're just as alone as I am, or you wouldn't be here right now."

"Well, I—" she started, but Finn only shook his head.

"If you'd had anywhere else to go, you would've when you ran into trouble." He regarded her coolly. "So tell me, Angel, why don't you have a loving family to run home to?"

"I do. Sort of," she said stiffly. This was not her favorite topic of conversation. "As it happens, I have perfectly nice parents and a whole pack of brothers. But I'm not the same sort of person they are. They just don't like me. End of discussion."

"That's how I feel about mine, too. Big difference, huh?"

"Look, my parents were fine. There was nothing terrible in my upbringing. They're perfectly nice people who just don't happen to share my view of the world, that's all." Defensive and frustrated, she smacked her hand into the arm of a chair nearby. "They thought I was too noisy and too greedy and just plain weird. And just because they weren't rich, it didn't make them paragons of virtue, okay?"

"They were farmers, weren't they?"

"Yes," she said without flinching. "And I know in your book that probably makes them wonderful, salt-of-the earth, hard-working, God-fearing people. And they were. But they weren't real fun to be around. And they weren't what I wanted in my life."

"So where are you going, Angel, when you get what you want and you get away from here? Do you go back where you came from, trading in your Chevy for a BMW, piling up a few more savings bonds?"

"I don't know. I hadn't thought about it," she lied.

"That's what I thought," he returned. "You're planning on leaving at the first sign of daylight—it's safe for you to go back, you're out of here, right? It's real easy to offer advice to other people when you don't intend to stick around and see if that advice holds water."

"What if I'm not?"

"Not what?"

"Leaving, necessarily."

"You, Miss Big Time, stick around a farm? Yeah, right."

"Well, I might," she countered. "Not forever, but for a while. What if I promise not to leave, to at least give some time to the farm and the kids? Will that convince you that I can put my money where my mouth is?"

"Then you and I have a date to attend to."

"You'll leave the farm long enough for a date?"

"You'll stay long enough to give the quiet life a chance?"

"I'll stay."

"Then I'll leave," he returned.

She wasn't sure if she'd just won the battle or lost the war. "I guess I'd better call Floyd," she said softly. "We're going to need a baby-sitter."

A DATE! WHAT HAD SHE agreed to? She felt like she was going to need a prom dress and a corsage—high school all over again.

Even if it wasn't high school, she was desperate for something to wear and some help with her hair. She still hadn't really figured out how to deal with its mass, and although she knew it was idiotic, she wanted to look right for her date.

In a weak moment, Angie asked very politely if she could use the truck to go into town.

"I'm not running away," she assured him when she saw the weary look on his face. "I'd like to get my hair cut, and maybe hit the mall. Layla says that's the only place to shop."

"Take Layla with you," he said gruffly, flipping her the keys.

"Does Layla need a shopping trip?"

"I don't know." His lips formed a semblance of a smile. "But that way, there's someone along to make sure you don't get into trouble."

"Great." Shrugging into one of Finn's collection of battered leather jackets, Angie propped open the back door and hitched Contessa Bibi's alligator bag, now carrying the dregs of her cash, over her shoulder.

"Oh, and Angel?"

"What?"

"Don't cut your hair."

She considered a moment. "We'll see." She grinned at him. "Maybe I'll come back with a whole new look."

Before he could answer, she set off for the girls' bunkhouse to find Layla.

The trip seemed to take forever, and Angie was amazed at just how far out of town they really were. After one gravel road rutted with ice, they hit black-top and finally a highway. At last they got to the mall, where Layla towed her around from one kicky juniors' shop to another.

"The sweatshirt with the hearts all over it is perfect for you, sweetie," Angie said wearily. "Look, I'll buy you that and the glow-green headband and the Christmas-bell earrings, too, but that's it."

"Super!"

As Layla raced for the checkout counter before her very own Lady Bountiful changed her mind, Angie asked, "Is there any store a little...more for me? Like someplace I could buy a silk blouse or a cashmere sweater?"

"What's catch-mer?"

"Never mind," Angie said with a sigh. She had enough cash to cover Layla's purchases, but it was going to be tight after that. What was she going to buy herself to wear? As she slipped the almost-empty wallet back into the alligator purse, her fingers brushed the place in the lining where she'd stuck her American Express card.

"I could charge it," she murmured. But how dangerous were credit cards when it came to tracing people?

"Come on, Angel," Layla prompted, grabbing her hand. "There's an old lady place on the over side, down by the toy store. Maybe your catch-mer thingy will be there. And then will you buy me a pretzel?"

"Sure," she answered with a smile, letting herself be dragged along. Mentally, she was still back on the charge-card problem. If she used it, would they find her? And how fast?

"Well, they didn't find me after I called Gretchen," she mused. "Besides, they won't know I wasn't just passing through. I mean, this mall's not even that close to Heavenly Acres. It might tell them where I was, but it won't tell them where I *am*."

Feeling much better, she sent Layla off to the toy store while she perused the racks at a very nice boutique.

"Ahhh," she breathed, fingering silk for the first time in ages. "Even if I get caught, it's worth it."

HER HAIR WAS FRESHLY shampooed and dried, with a new barrette twisted into the back to keep the wispy tendrils out of her face. She had patted it twelve or thirteen times to make sure it was holding okay back there. So far, so good.

Angie checked her lipstick again in the bathroom mirror. Good grief! It was the first time she'd worn makeup since she'd hit Heavenly Acres. Now that she was a blonde, her colors were all different, and she'd had to play around with blushers and shadows to get it to look good.

But in her new ice-pink silk blouse, with tiny pink pearl earrings that only cost her two dollars at one of Layla's favorite stores, she did look good. She was convinced. Almost.

Angie had washed her jeans just for tonight, deciding that a skirt or nice pants would be too dressy for a date with a man who pretended not to know the meaning of "altruistic." Besides, those kinds of outfits required panty hose and nice shoes, and she wasn't in the mood to pop for all that. She'd already broken down and bought a winter coat, for goodness' sake, since she simply couldn't bear that fur thing. More damage to her American Express, but the winter-white wool coat was perfect.

So here she was, in silk and denim, snow-white coat over her arm, trying to calm down before she saw Finn. Poor man. Ever since she'd appropriated his bedroom, she had no idea where he was dressing and showering and all that.

"Angel? You up there?" a deep voice called from the bottom of the stairs.

Her heart did an extra bounce or two before she realized it had too much of a hick accent to be Finn. "Floyd," she concluded. The baby-sitter had arrived.

Floyd's gunmetal-gray crew cut was bristling with authority as he stood at attention in the living room. "So," he rumbled, "you and Finn taking off tonight, huh?"

"Yes, that's right." She chewed her lip. "You haven't seen Finn by any chance, have you?"

"Naah." He jerked a thumb toward the rear of the house. "Probably out back in the boys' bunkhouse, laying down the law. He don't like to leave the little heathens alone, y'know. First time I can recall Finn taking off except to pick up a new kid. No, sir, he don't like leaving them kids alone at night."

"I know. I kind of talked him into it." Angie added, "But you will be all right with them tonight, won't you? I mean, this is all okay, right?"

"A-okay," Floyd shot back like a drill sergeant. "Yessir, them kids will be hopping to with ol' Floyd on their tails." A fierce light glowed in his iron-gray eyes. "I ain't taking no nonsense."

Oh dear. It sounded as bad as Finn had predicted. Floyd would rule with an iron hand, the kids would rebel, and there would be sheer chaos by the time they returned. "Well, let's look on the bright side," she said in as cheerful a tone as she could manage. "Maybe they'll all be on their best behavior."

"Their best ain't none too good," Floyd said sourly. "Well, I'll be seeing you. I got some exercises I want those kids doing, and I better get the lead out."

"Right."

The butterflies in her stomach began to dance the polka. This was all her idea, and if it was a disaster, everyone would know who to blame. Angie Marie Boone, aka Politico's Sex Kitten, aka Angel. Might as well take the photos for the mug shot.

The back door flipped open and Angie really started to panic. Finn? Would he still go along with this? Or had he seen the error of both their ways? Or maybe the cops would arrive to arrest her because she'd weakened and used the damn credit card.

In a scenario right out of her worst fantasies, Finn walked in from the kitchen, accompanied by a pudgy uniformed cop. Heads together, they were talking intently and very quietly as they entered the living room.

Angie froze where she was, clasping and unclasping her hands, waiting to hear her own death sentence.

"This is her," Finn announced, and she just about went through the floor. "Angel, I'd like you to meet a friend of mine. This is Sergeant Melvin Sibley, from the Champaign Police Department."

"Nice to meet you, ma'am," he said, sticking out a hand and eyeing Angie very curiously. "Finn's told me a lot about you."

She tried to regain her composure. "Oh, well, wasn't that nice of him?" she asked hastily. "It's a pleasure, umm, Sergeant."

"Melvin was just leaving," Finn remarked, watching her carefully as he spoke. "He stopped by to check in with me about something."

"Yep, that's right." The burly sergeant cut a path toward the front door, calling out behind him, "Sorry I didn't bring you anything, Finn. If I hear anything, you'll be the first to know."

"Thanks, Mel."

"No prob," he said, and he saluted as he marched out the door.

"So," Finn muttered.

He jammed his hands in the pockets of his trousers, and Angie noticed suddenly that he wasn't wearing jeans. Except for the ratty gym shorts, this was the first time she'd seen him in anything but blue jeans. In fact, he looked terrific. Clean-shaven, in a crisp white shirt and black pants, he looked better than terrific. Mouth-watering. Fabulous. Absolutely amazing. Trust Finn to clean up like a million bucks. Angie swallowed and pulled her eyes away.

"You ready to go?" he asked quietly.

"Uh, yes," she answered. "I saw Floyd, so he's here, so that's all set, and I'm, umm, all set, so I guess we're..."

"All set," Finn finished for her.

"Right."

"Then let's get out of here."

He held open the door for her, and then helped her climb up into the truck. It was all very civil, but also very odd. The tension between them was palpable, and it seemed to have affected both their tongues.

As he put the key in the ignition, Finn commented gruffly, "You look good in pink."

She could've sworn he hadn't so much as glanced at her attire before she'd put on her coat, so how did he know what color her blouse was underneath it?

"Thanks," she said awkwardly. "You look very nice yourself. I wasn't sure whether I should wear something more dressy, and maybe I should've, since you're more dressed up than I am, but I thought jeans would be okay, and I hope you didn't plan on going anywhere really dressy or anything. You didn't, did you? Plan on somewhere dressy?"

Finn's gaze narrowed. "Do you always talk this much when you're nervous?"

"Who said I was nervous?"

"It isn't hard to figure out."

"Well, maybe I am a bit nervous. I can't remember the last time I went on a date, I mean, that somebody actually called a date."

He frowned. "What do they call it where you come from?"

"Anything noncommittal, you know, like, 'Want to do dinner sometime?' I think my last date said, 'Listen, I have two tickets to the Kennedy Center. Want to share a cab?'"

She'd made her voice nasal and whiny on purpose to be amusing, as well as to give him an indication of the character of the moron she'd gone out with, but she felt like the whole thing fell flat. She was talking too much and saying nothing, and Finn was biting bullets over on his side of the front seat.

"Kennedy Center, huh? As in, Washington, D.C.?"

There was no point in denying it. "That would, uh, be the one," she murmured.

She hadn't even noticed that little slip before Finn pointed it out. Heavens, she was getting sloppy, and she didn't have the wherewithal to care anymore, either. So Finn knew where she'd been; at this rate, it was only a matter of time before she spilled the whole thing, anyway. And so what? So what if Finn was filling in all the details that drew her portrait?

In some strange way, in some defiant part of her soul, she realized she wanted him to know everything about her. It was no longer a question of *if* she'd tell him about Lance and the whole mess, but when.

Looking out into the vast expanse of Illinois farmland visible through her window, she had a funny feeling of déjà vu. "How funny," she said, letting her mind wander to the past. "I had a date once before in a truck. I just remembered. It was the Homecoming dance my senior year in high school, and Billy McGraw asked me. He lived on the farm next to my parents'—nice, clean-cut boy, Future Farmers of America, the whole nine yards. So of course I hated his guts."

"Of course," Finn said softly.

"But nobody else asked me, so my dad said I had to go with Billy." She laughed. "It was awful. I think I spent the whole date looking out the window."

"Is that what you're going to do tonight?"

When she glanced over at Finn, her memories of Billy McGraw and the Homecoming from Hell vanished abruptly. He wasn't doing anything special, just sitting over there on his side, one wrist dangling over the top of the steering wheel, driving into the night. But somehow, looking at him, her mouth went dry, and her fantasies kicked into high gear. There was no way to fill up the hot, dark silence that separated them, not with nonstop words, not with fuzzy recollections of bygone days.

Angie's mind played back the sensual memories of the first time she'd ridden in Finn's truck. Once again, her nose took in the scent of worn leather and warm, clean man, as her eyes lingered on the chiseled perfection of his profile and marked the small white scar slicing his right eyebrow. His mouth was a curious mixture of cruelty and vulnerability, and her fingers ached to trace its lines.

It was cold in the truck—it was always cold in the truck—but when she shivered, it had nothing to do with the temperature.

"Finn," she began, and her voice came out husky and strained. She looked away, but she could still feel him with every breath that she took, as though the air in the small space between them had become heavy, shadowed, singed with electricity. The question haunting her was one she knew she shouldn't ask, but she couldn't hold it back. "Finn," she said again, taking her time with the feel of his name on her lips. "What were you planning on happening between us tonight?"

As her words reached him, his jaw clenched and his hands tightened on the wheel. "I changed my mind," he said roughly.

Suddenly, he slammed on the brakes and veered the truck off the side of the desolate road, wrenching it to a stop under the bare branches of a huge oak tree. Around them, there was only darkness and the hoot of an owl.

Finn stared straight ahead, out his windshield into the black night. "I'm not in the mood for food," he said darkly. "And neither are you. There's just one thing we both want, and we can do it here a lot better than we can in the middle of a restaurant."

She was afraid to ask, but there was no turning back now. "What one thing?"

''This,'' he said roughly, reaching over and pulling her up into his lap in the cramped confines of the front seat.

And then, with hunger in his eyes, he covered her mouth with his.

Chapter Eleven

Her new coat and his leather jacket slithered to the floor together, the first casualties of the escalating passion inside Finn's truck.

"Angel," he breathed, holding her hard inside the circle of his arms, trailing kisses down her neck and inside the slinky collar of her blouse.

She didn't waste time on words, just angled farther into his lap and wrapped her arms around him, opening her mouth into his kiss. If it had been chilly inside the pickup, it was warm and toasty now. As her head tipped to one side to allow Finn's kisses, Angie closed her eyes, but she'd already seen the windows steaming over.

She couldn't quite believe they were doing this, making out in the front seat like overheated teenagers, but it felt so good, she was in no position to complain. After wanting this man for so long, after denying it for so long, she was ready to explode into flames. If this was her one chance, Angie Marie Boone planned to grab it.

"Take this off," she said urgently, pushing at his shirt, tearing at the buttons, needing to feel his skin under her hands before sanity returned and she changed her mind.

And when she had succeeded in separating him from the shirt, she laid her hands flat against the warm, smooth expanse of his wonderful chest. Shameless, she slid her cheek against his strong muscles, exulting in the sensation. Her hands glided over his shoulders and his back, kneading him, urging him closer, as she branded him with the wettest, hottest kisses she could deliver.

But it wasn't until she trailed tendrils of her hair over his bare shoulders, letting it tickle and torment him as it drifted across, that she really knew he was as far gone as she was.

"Angel," he whispered hoarsely, thrusting his hands deep into the heavy waves of her hair, rubbing the strands between his fingers and across his cheek.

Edging back into the depths of the seat, she tried to pull Finn with her, to maneuver both of them into a more horizontal position. Unfortunately, the steering wheel, most of her hair, and their discarded clothes kept getting in the way. But Angie didn't care. Finn shoved what he could aside as they tumbled headlong into the seat, a force of nature that the truck was simply going to have to make room for.

Full out, with the hard length of his body nestled against her, Angie felt flushed and feverish, as though someone were lighting matches and tickling her with the flames. He was smashed up into the seat, and she was falling over the edge, but it didn't matter in the least.

He kissed her again, brushing his lips across the corners of her mouth, her chin, down the slope of her neck to her collarbone. He raised a hand to her top button, and then he hesitated.

His blue eyes scorched her; he held her with his wild, lambent gaze. "Are you sure?"

"Yes."

Her eyes never left his. Trembling, she slipped her hands over his, guiding his fingers as they slid the button through the hole. One button and then the next...the flutter of silk against her skin, against his...the sizzling, sultry feel of his breath as his mouth traced an erotic pattern down her shoulders and her breasts.

Restless, she lay trembling under his clever fingers and his mouth, afraid to do anything that might put an end to this mindless bliss. Moving down slowly, he lowered his lips to her breasts, wetting her nipples through their thin lace covering, circling them with his tongue, biting down ever so gently, until she thought she would go mad with desire.

"No more, please." Even as her body arched up into his mouth, she begged, "Please, Finn, I can't take this."

"Yes, you can," he said, in the raw silk voice of the devil himself. "We're just getting started."

But she knew how to put an end to his damned control. She tangled a leg around him, pulling herself closer, until she could press her lower body hard against the front of his jeans, back and forth, and he groaned out loud.

He wore no belt, and she undid the top button of his pants before he could hold her back.

"Not so fast," he whispered, trying to catch her fingers, but she eluded his grasp.

"Be quiet," she told him. "Kiss me." Nipping at his lips, she caught the back of his neck with one hand, pressing him to kiss her hard and deep. With her other hand, she found his zipper, slithering it down before he could interfere. She could hear the insistent chink of metal links; the small sound reverberated inside her, pushing her beyond the point of sense or sensibility.

And then she reached down, slipping inside the front of his trousers, reaching for him. Her fingers brushed the warm, hard velvet....

"Wait," he said roughly, rotating his hips away as he lifted his head and took a few ragged breaths. He braced himself on one arm, using the other one to pin Angie's wayward hand at the wrist. "One second."

Angie was in no mood to wait. She was out of her mind with wanting him. "I'm not waiting," she told him. "No more."

"Insistent little thing, aren't you?"

"Yeah." She smiled wickedly as she dragged him back by the belt loops. "Come on, Finn. Stop playing hard to get."

"A half-naked man in the front seat of a pickup is not what I'd call playing hard to get."

"Oh, yeah?" She raised herself up far enough to nip his lower lip. "Then what are you waiting for?"

His lips curved in a rakish smile. "Not a damn thing," he murmured, and he reached for the snap of her jeans.

It was tough maneuvering around in the slippery confines of the front seat, sliding off the seat, smashing into the door handles, and almost falling into the gearshift three or four times. But neither one was willing to give in to minor obstacles like those.

Until finally, there she was, ragged and breathless, waiting for Finn.

"You are sure about his, aren't you?" he asked softly. His eyes were dark with desire, and with some other emotion she didn't want to deal with right now.

"I'm sure." Her hands around his hard, strong hips, she coaxed him nearer.

He smiled again, with a soft, sexy, pleasure-filled grin that stole her heart away. "Angel," he whispered, and then he covered her body with his.

She arched up to meet him, pulling him inside with the force of her need. "Yes," she urged. "Oh, yes."

She had never felt so complete, so sated and so unbelievably hungry, all at the same time. Finn was everything she'd ever wanted, and she held on to his sweat-slick body with all her might as they rode the waves of passion together.

Stroking her, whispering to her, covering her skin with his kisses, he plunged inside again and again, wild and hot and strong, until the fire raged too far out of control to hold back.

"Angel," he cried, as they reached the crest together.

His arms still encircled her, holding her fast, as she struggled to find words. Who needed words at a time like this? Her whole life had changed in the front seat of a pickup. She started to giggle.

"You're laughing?" he asked, with an incredulous tone.

"I can't believe it," she murmured, drawing his head down to kiss him full on the lips. "We just made love in a truck."

"I wish it could have been different." His voice dropped into a husky register. "You deserve better, Angel."

"Oh, I enjoyed it," she told him with a sly smile. "I definitely enjoyed it."

Before he could ask any questions about their future or the impact of what they'd shared, Angie pressed her lips to his. She didn't want to think about the future; she just wanted to enjoy the moment. Lying in Finn's arms, she wanted to lie back and look at the stars, do all those goofy things lovers did. Once the steam cleared from the windows, of course.

As if reading her mind, Finn leaned over her to crank open the window a bit. "A little air," he murmured, brushing a kiss on her forehead. "I think we both need a little air." Then he settled back on top of her, bracketing her face with his hands, smiling at her as he bit the top of her nose. "Now, where were we?"

"Mmm." She shifted so she could see out the front window. "The stars are beautiful here," she said dreamily. "It's so strange to be able to see so many. Should I make a wish? But which one did I see first?"

"Angel," he began, in a very strained voice, "do you smell smoke?"

Angie sniffed. "Smoke."

"I definitely smell smoke." Finn opened his door and leaned out into the night air, angling for a better view. "Flames," he said tersely, vaulting back into his seat and scrambling to find his shirt. "There are flames coming from the direction of Heavenly Acres. Damn it all to hell, I think they're burning down the farm."

"What?" She was toasty from the fire they'd created, but it had nothing to do with Heavenly Acres. "Are you sure?"

"Of course I'm sure," Finn said testily, revving up the engine and shoving his arms into his shirt at the same time. "I never should've left them alone. I knew this would happen."

"So are we going back to the farm now?"

"Yes," he said impatiently. "So you'd better get dressed in a hurry."

"I can't find my—oh, hell, there it is."

"Damn it, Angel, you're swearing again."

"So are you."

As the pickup jolted along the rutted road, she tossed his jacket at him without looking, and scrambled to button her blouse over breasts that were still wet from Finn's mouth. She was freezing, but her body still flamed from Finn's touch and Finn's embrace. She felt tender and sore all over, but she didn't know if it was from their energetic lovemaking or from the obstacle course in the front seat. She was too old for this kind of vehicular misconduct.

"Put your clothes on," he said fiercely. "We're almost there."

"I'm trying!"

Dragging her coat over her arms, she fastened it all the way up to her neck so that no one would see that the buttons and buttonholes on her blouse didn't match up right. It wasn't her fault. The truck kept bouncing, and her hands were amazingly uncoordinated.

"Do you really think the farm's on fire?" she asked, peering out the windshield.

"The farm, the barns, the animals...the kids. Could be none of it—could be all of it," he said bleakly.

"Oh, Finn. What will we do?"

A stiff winter wind blew the clouds of smoke around through the trees, obscuring the point of origin somewhat, but she could still see the orange-red glow of flames lighting up the darkness, just far enough away to be Heavenly Acres.

"I knew something terrible would happen if I left," Finn muttered. "They probably gave Floyd trouble, and then he ordered laps around the barn or marine push-ups or something. I can just see Zero tying the old coot to a chair and setting the bunkhouse on fire."

"Zero wouldn't do that," Angie said doubtfully.

"Just try him." He pressed down harder on the accelerator, making the old truck lunge and cough.

"Slow down! Do you want to get there in one piece or a lot of little ones?"

"I never should've left them alone," he repeated.

"Why don't we save the speeches until after we know how bad it is?"

But in her heart of hearts, Angie knew upon whose shoulders blame would be placed. She was the one who'd bullied him into leaving the farm, she was the one who'd convinced him that Floyd could handle the kids, and she was the one who was going to be blamed for any atrocities Zero and his pals had committed.

She was still so turned on she couldn't sit still, yet at the same time, so miserable she wanted to curl up on the seat of the pickup and never speak to anyone again. Especially not Finn.

"Are you decent?" he asked grimly. She could hear the fear suppressed in his voice. "We're here."

Without slowing down more than a millimeter, he spun the wheel and brought the truck bolting through an ever-thickening cloud of smoke and blowing embers, up the gravel driveway, finally squealing to a stop next to the house. And then he jumped from the truck, leaving his door hanging open as he dashed toward the flames behind the house.

Choking and coughing, Angie followed, fighting her way through the fumes. "Where are you?" she called out. "I can't see anything."

"Right here," Finn's voice replied, sounding not so much scared anymore as bemused.

"Why do you sound so... Oh."

Following the direction of his voice, she'd broken out into clear air, upwind of the fire. And that's when she saw what he saw, and when she realized why his voice had lost that savage edge.

There was no massive conflagration, no out-of-control blaze threatening the bunkhouses or the barn or anything else. Instead, there was only a bonfire. It was a big bonfire, but a bonfire, nonetheless. Burning leaves, from the looks of it. Around the fire, the hardened, streetwise children of Heavenly Acres were roasting weenies and toasting marshmallows. They were surrounded by tents and sleeping bags and all the paraphernalia of a Boy Scout Jamboree.

She scanned the crowd for Zero, the resident troublemaker, but he was perfectly happily occupied, with his leather half gloves wrapped around the cool end of a pointed stick. From this distance, she couldn't tell if he had a hot dog or a marshmallow, or if he was just burning up a stick, but he didn't seem to be getting into anything too dangerous.

"Not exactly what I expected," Angie mumbled.

"Greetings," Floyd growled, advancing on them with a General Patton pipe in his mouth. "Early evening, eh?"

Finn was completely silent, so Angie took the opportunity. "What is all this?"

"Camp out," he barked. "Kids need to know how to camp out—good for 'em. Outdoors, fresh air, ghost stories—put some hair on their chests."

"Right," Finn said. He still sounded sort of in shock.

"So everything is going okay?" Angie inquired. "No mutiny? No misbehavior?"

Floyd's crew cut bristled with disapproval. "Not a bit," he declared, chomping down on the stem of his pipe. "What do you take me for, little lady? Think I'd stand for mutiny or misbehavior?"

"Well, everything certainly looks fine. Don't you think so, Finn?" She elbowed him to get an answer.

"Uh, right," he said, wandering off a bit to gauge this strange behavior up closer.

"Carry on," Floyd ordered. "Don't need you here. All-night camp out." He gave Angie a meaningful wink. "I'll be patrolling all night—make sure they're all in their bunks and accounted for. All night."

"Oh, I see." Angie winked back. "Thanks, Floyd. You're doing a great job."

He cleared his throat. "You, uh, might want to make sure Finn buttons his shirt and zips up his, uh, trousers, if you're planning on seeing anyone this evening. Looks a tad suspicious in that condition."

As he gave her a jaunty salute and went back to his charges, Angie tried not to blush. Without explanation, she caught Finn by the arm, dragging him back through the worst part of the smoke to the truck.

"You didn't put yourself back together properly, you nitwit. Floyd knew exactly what we'd been up to, and so did most of the kids, if they got a gander at you." She slammed the driver's door on the truck with authority. "I know you were worried, but this is ridiculous."

"Look, I'm sorry," he offered stiffly. His dark brows lowered in the middle as he gazed at her. "For assuming the worst, I mean."

"Oh, that's okay." Leaning over, Angie couldn't resist zipping up the front of his leather jacket. Wouldn't want him to catch cold. "Who expected

Floyd to turn this place into a Norman Rockwell painting?''

"You did.''

"No, I didn't.'' Since he was being so kind as to apologize, she could afford to be a little magnanimous in return. "I was just as scared as you were. More scared. I knew if something bad happened, it would be my fault.''

He shook his head. "Your fault? Give yourself a break, Angel.'' With a renewal of his usual moxie, he glanced over at her with a touch of mischief in his blue eyes. "Do you know what we were doing when we were so rudely interrupted?''

"Looking at the stars?'' she asked hopefully.

"Maybe that's what you were looking at. I had a better view of a celestial body.'' He draped an arm around her shoulders and guided her around toward the front door. "Want to try to recreate the scenario?''

"Not in the front seat I don't.''

"I wasn't thinking about the truck.'' Edging around to face her, he lifted her chin with one finger and then just stood there, watching her. "We have an empty house and a few hours to kill. What do you think?''

"Well, this was supposed to be your night to blow off steam,'' she said carefully, casually. "I guess we might as well make the most of it. And it would be a shame to waste this whole, long, empty evening.'' She paused. "Wouldn't it?''

His lazy smile took her breath away. "A real shame.''

And then he swung her up into his arms and carried her past the sign of the Angel, in the front door of his house and up the stairs to his bedroom.

"Ever since you got here, I've been imagining you in my bed," he told her. "Looks like my imagination is about to pay off."

IT WAS DIFFERENT NOW, not like being caught up in the first rush of desire too strong to deny. This was a tryst born of reflection, of calmer moments, of two people deciding with cool heads and cool bodies that they wanted to share their lives and their love.

In a strange way, Finn reflected as he stepped out of the shower and wrapped a towel around his waist, it was like a honeymoon night. Not that he was planning on mentioning that to Angel.

But when he slid into the cool sheets beside her, dropping his towel to the floor next to the bed, her beautiful blond hair tumbled around them, and the dainty nightgown that he'd bought her slipped off one shoulder, revealing the warm, pale tones of her sweet, sweet skin . . . Finn knew in his heart exactly what this was, even if they'd never speak the words aloud.

"Much nicer here than in the damned truck."

He smiled gently at her, hoping to allay any awkwardness. Now that their wild, fearless passion was spent, it was more difficult to justify coming together on softer, saner terms. Things had changed between them, and these were trickier waters to navigate.

What would she do if she knew he was as scared as she was? At least she had a nightgown to hide in. Beside her, he was buck naked, and already hard with wanting.

Slow, he told himself. *Gotta go slow this time.*

"You trust me, don't you?" he asked softly, brushing the gentlest of kisses over her mouth, carefully keeping the lower, more impatient part of his body on his own side of the bed.

"Of course," she said with a smile.

"I need to know your name, Angel. Your real name. Can you tell me who you are?"

"My name is Angie," she whispered.

"Angie. So close to Angel." His kisses moved to her forehead, her cheeks. "But you still look like an angel to me."

"I'm no angel, Finn." He could feel her smile next to his mouth as she said the words, and he tried to hold back the fierce joy he was feeling. He hugged her tightly, signaling some small part of his emotions.

"I was born and raised in Nebraska," she went on, in the same husky, breathless tone, as she settled herself against him in a rustle of lace and fine white cotton. "And I have six younger brothers."

Her gown was tickling him, tantalizing him, brushing against the very part of him that needed no invitation to jump to attention. *Slow down,* he commanded himself.

"Six?" he murmured, bestowing six more kisses, tracing a path behind her ear and down to her adorable shoulder.

"We're alphabetical," she murmured, closing her eyes and leaning into his embrace. "Angie, Bob, Carl,

Darryl, Eddie, Frank and Gary. Do I get a prize for remembering all of them?''

"I thought I was the prize."

"You'll do." She touched his cheek and then his eyebrow, tracing the slim, white scar etched into his brow. "You'll do just fine."

"Thanks," he said in the barest of whispers, playing with the thin white strap of her nightgown where it threatened to fall completely off her shoulder. As he pressed his lips to that sweet spot, cherishing every inch of her skin, she held on to the bodice of the nightgown, keeping it secure for the moment. He had no intention of leaving it that way for long.

"Do you have any brothers or sisters, Finn?" she asked in a slow, seductive voice that told him she had other things besides his siblings on her mind.

"An older brother. Ten years older," he replied, dropping his voice low and drawing out every word as he touched her, caressed her, torturing her with his leisurely pace, the same way she was torturing him. He smiled as he filled one hand with her hair, edging it out of the way so he could nibble her ear. "But we're not alphabetical. Welles is his name. Haven't seen old Welles since I was sixteen."

She slid her tongue over his lips, and then backed off when he would've deepened the kiss. He could tell from the naughty gleam in her eye that she intended to keep things at a snail's pace, no matter how often either of them was tempted to go a little faster.

"So you really were born with a silver spoon in that gorgeous mouth of yours?" she asked lazily, fingering his upper lips.

"More like a whole silver service." It wasn't something he cared to think about, especially at a time like this. "Angry kid—that was me. They didn't know what to do with me."

"Like Zero, huh?"

"A whole lot worse than Zero." No need to go into those faraway misdeeds. He wasn't the same person as that terrible, miserable kid, the one who'd run away from home, or stolen and cheated and punched his way off the streets. "Let's just say I reformed, shall we?"

He pushed her back into the sheets. "Enough talking." He gave her his most ruthless smile. "Actions speak louder."

And then he pulled down the loose straps of the nightgown, revealing her beautiful breasts to his rapt gaze. "Angel," he breathed, and he bent to kiss the pink crests of her breasts. Stroking, caressing, lavishing care on her sweet, succulent skin, he tried to go slow, but he knew it was a losing battle.

Small sounds of pleasure escaped her, and she began to writhe under his mouth. "Ohh, Finn," she whispered, the syllables escaping her as a shallow sigh. She tried to push her gown away, and pull him in, wrapping her legs around his hips. "I need you now, Finn. I feel awful and lonely and *wonderful*. Can you please come inside?"

"Shh," he soothed, swiftly unwrapping her from the folds of the nightgown, stripping away fabric until she was as naked and vulnerable as he was, and there was nothing between them but the combined warmth of bare skin.

He embraced her tightly for a long moment, absorbing her trembling with the solid weight of his much larger, much longer body. He wanted to enfold her with his warmth, hold her close and safe within his arms. Protective. He felt protective, when the only thing she'd need to be protected from was he and his raging lust.

Her small hands pulled him nearer. Against him, he could feel her melting and tightening, pulsing under his fingers; she was ready for him, and with everything he had, he was ready for her.

"Please, now," she begged, reaching for him, taking his hard, hot length in her hand. "Now."

There was no way to hold out against that kind of enticement. He ran his hands lovingly, wonderingly, over her smooth, round bottom, as he positioned her underneath him and plunged inside. She was so hot and wet and perfect, he felt like he was losing his mind.

She was moving underneath him, sheathing him and holding him, and he tried to slow down, to make it last. But it was too late. Much too late for finesse.

He had never had a problem with control before, never had a problem holding on until the exact moment he was ready to let go. But now, for the second time in one night, he had no choice. The pleasure was so intense, his body seemed to be moving and stroking of its own accord, and Angel's incoherent little moans only drove him higher. He inched his fingertips down between them, touching, grazing her most sensitive, secret place, needing to bring her to the same hard peak of ecstasy he was feeling.

"Finn," she murmured, with a hunger he could well understand. "Finn," she cried again, louder, and he felt her desire tighten and break free under his fingers.

Desperately, he lost himself inside her, whispering the word "Angel" as the tide swept him away.

And then he held her fast against his sweat-slick chest, too tired and sated and just plain happy to move.

Smiling like the Cheshire cat, Angel rolled over on top of him and painted his face with soft kisses. "I'll never forget you, Finn. Never."

Cradling her in his arms, he drifted to sleep, although he did have occasion to wonder, through the soft gray haze of his exhaustion, why she had chosen those words for this particular moment. "Ask her in the morning," he mumbled, twining one hand through the expanse of her hair and cuddling in closer. "Ask her in the morning."

Chapter Twelve

JoJo "the Mongoose" Mando was jubilant. It was difficult for outsiders to figure that out, because JoJo was pretty darned fearsome to look at, one way or the other. But his employer, Mr. Lou "Elevator Man" Anthony, knew that a certain twinkle in those beady eyes, a kind of spring in that lumbering stride, could mean only one thing.

The Elevator Man glanced up from his massage table. "Eh, JoJo, you found the broad, am I right?" he asked between whacks from his Norwegian masseur.

"Aw, Mr. Anthony, you can read me like a book." The big ox dipped his head in disappointment. "I wanted to break it to you myself, Mr. A. You spoiled the surprise."

"Olaf, take a powder," Lou Anthony barked, struggling to a sitting position and waving off the Norwegian.

"Yah, sure, Mr. Antony," the masseur responded quickly. "You need me, you yust call, yah?" Grabbing his towels and his lotions, he was gone in a flash.

"So, gimme it," the Elevator Man ordered. "Where is she? How soon we got her and my money in our hands, uh?"

"She was one dumb broad, Mr. A." JoJo shook his massive head back and forth with disbelief. "Used her charge card yesterday. We was watching those cards like a hawk, and whammo! We got her."

"Where, JoJo?"

"Someplace... Lemme see here." Gingerly, JoJo pulled a small slip of paper out of his pocket, holding it up between stubby fingers. "Champaign, Illinois. Zat where they make the bubbly, huh?"

"No, that ain't where they make no bubbly. That's in California, you dummy."

"Oh, yeah, sorry, Mr. A. Anyway, about the broad. She used her American Express card yesterday, twice, two stores at the same mall—signatures match, so it ain't just stolen cards or nothing. So we matched up this Champaign place with them phone numbers we stole from the feds. And whammo! One of them's only ten miles away from the mall. Yeah," he said happily, losing his neck into the folds of his shirt as he tried to smile, "we got her, Mr. A. We got the broad, fair and square."

"What do I care about fair and square?" snarled the boss. "Get to the broad, JoJo, and find my money. And then, you know what to do."

JoJo's eyes gleamed with anticipation. "Ya mean I get to off her? I like offing broads."

"I know, JoJo." Mr. Anthony stretched himself back out on the table. "Get outta here, will ya? And send Olaf back in. I got this crick in my neck. Must be stress, huh?''

"Yeah, Mr. A. You bet.''

JoJo strutted out the door, already feeling the broad's skinny neck snap between his hands. He sure did love offing broads.

"Mmm," SHE SAID, unwilling to give up the drowsy, cozy pleasure of sleeping next to Finn. She snuggled closer to his chest and pretended she was still asleep.

"How are you this morning?" he asked, feathering kisses along her hairline.

"Mmm," she murmured again, winding a leg around his. "I'm really, *really* fine."

"Are you?"

"Oh, yes."

She gave him a lopsided smile and tried not to feel shy. They'd had more together last night than she'd known it was possible to share with a man. She traced his scar with her finger, contemplating these new feelings. Tenderness, confusion, vulnerability, maybe even love. No, she told herself, that was leftover lust. There was a lot of that left around to contend with.

He was still Finn, of course, still Mr. Tough Guy, but as she surveyed the cool, enigmatic cast to his features, she knew he was different now. Now he was *her* Mr. Tough Guy, with the fragrance of her hair clinging to his skin, with the scent of her body mingled with his.

"Angie?" he asked.

It was very strange hearing that name on his lips. From the curious light in his eyes, she had a feeling she was about to undergo a more serious interrogation. "Yes?" she asked, with more than a bit of trepidation.

"Was there a man?"

"A man?" she echoed.

"The reason you ran away, was it a man?"

She tried to smooth away the black expression from his brow. "No, no man was involved," she lied. It was what he wanted to hear; it was what she wanted to tell him.

"So what was it? Why did you run?"

"I was accused of stealing," she said reluctantly. "There was no way to get out of it, no way to tell the truth and make anyone believe me." She searched his face. "But you believe me, don't you, Finn?"

"Sure." He kissed her quickly. "I'll always be on your side."

"I know you probably think I should've stayed and tried to fight, but I had no choice," she insisted. "I couldn't just sit there and take the blame for something I didn't do. I had to leave, until they could find the person who really did it."

"Just simple theft? That's all?"

Crossing her fingers under the sheets, she answered, "That's all."

She already felt guilty for keeping things back, but how could she tell him the rest, about Lance and the FBI and the mob? She didn't even know what horrendous details they'd lined up against her. And then there was the "politico's sex kitten" business. She couldn't help hoping Finn would never have to know that part.

It wasn't that she didn't trust him, but more that she felt she'd hit the important thing. He didn't have to know the depth of her humiliation, did he?

"That's all," she repeated.

"And why couldn't you tell me this before?"

In a small voice, she said, "I didn't want you to think of me that way. As a criminal and a fake. My hair isn't even really blonde."

"I know."

"How do you...? Oh," she whispered, remembering last night. Of course he knew. "But it was dark in here. I didn't think you'd—"

"Come here." He sat up in the bed, dragging her with him. "Don't be embarrassed," he told her. "I don't care what color your hair is." A wicked grin curved his lips. "I'm just enjoying the chance to see all of it. In fact, I'd love to, uh, check it out again. Verify the color, so to speak."

"Oh, yeah," she whispered, linking her arms around his neck and sinking back into the bedclothes. "Better make sure."

"WE GOT TROUBLE," Jake Gannon announced with a frown. He slid into a chair and tossed a sheaf of papers at the other operative in the Angie Marie Boone command center.

Al rubbed his aching stomach and popped a few more antacids before examining the bad news. "What's this?"

"Olaf, our informant inside Elevator Man Anthony's operation, just called in. He overheard big doings at the Anthony compound early this morn-

ing—seems Anthony and his hoods have located Angie Marie Boone, and the muscle is already on the
way.''

Swearing loudly, Al reached for another handful of
antacids. ''Where is she, and how did those jokers find
her first?'' He slammed a fist into the table next to his
computer screen. ''Damn it, anyway. We had it down
to a list of forty-three names.''

''Well, find one near Champaign, Illinois,'' Jake
returned. ''That's where Olaf says JoJo the Mongoose is headed to rub out the Boone woman. She
used a credit card, and the Mongoose traced it, and
her, without even breaking a sweat.''

''Damn it,'' Al growled. ''There won't be anything
left but a few broken pieces by the time we get to her.''

''Okay, well, here's the only number in that part of
Illinois.'' Shaking his head grimly, Jake pointed to a
line near the bottom of the phone company's computer printout. ''Come on, Al, we've got to at least try
to keep her alive. It's a rural address, listed under the
name of Finn Sheridan.''

''All right, all right.'' Al shrugged. ''Get some op-
eratives down there from Chicago, or over from Indy,
whatever's closer. Tell them to keep an eye on this
place until we can fly in—''

''Got it,'' Jake returned, grabbing his jacket and his
gun. ''We're going to get her, Al. She may be a thief,
but she doesn't deserve what JoJo has in mind.''

''Nobody deserves what JoJo has in mind,'' Al retorted. ''Hell, Attila the Hun didn't deserve JoJo.''

"SO YOU FINALLY DECIDED to get up, huh?" Zero grumbled.

Angie really didn't need this this morning, but it looked like she was going to get it, anyway. Zero was hip-deep in his juvenile delinquent mode, complete with sullen pout and leather-fisted gloves. She ignored the rude question, offering a more polite query of her own. "Do you happen to know if Finn is around?"

"Nope. Went into town a while ago."

"Oh," she said with disappointment.

She'd hoped to be able to catch him this morning, to share a little more bliss, but he'd left while she was still sleeping off the effects of their most recent bout of lovemaking. Her cheeks flushed with warmth at the thought, although she certainly hoped Zero didn't notice.

"Do you know where he went?"

"Yes, I know where he went," Zero sassed back. He glowered at her under his sleepy lids. "He had a message from that fat cop pal of his to come into town right away and see him."

"I wonder what that was about."

Zero sneered. "Better hope it wasn't about you."

"And why would it have anything to do with me?" she asked slowly, calmly.

Her stomach dropped as Zero reached inside his jacket and pulled out a glossy weekly magazine.

"I'm s'posed to be doing a report for Finn on presidential politics," he spit out. "He thought it would be good for me—you know, write a whole paragraph or something. So I thought I'd pick up a mag. Get a real source, y'know? Only what I been reading ain't about politics."

He slapped the thing down on the kitchen table, revealing the cover illustration. It was she, and Angie went cold. Oddly enough, the cartoonish drawing looked more lifelike than any of the photographs she'd seen in the papers.

"The Hunt for Angie Marie Boone," the banner read. There was a slick drawing of her face and body, making her resemble a call girl a lot more than a mid-level bureaucrat, with little money bags piled behind her.

"So, sex kitten, tell me. How's it hangin'?" Zero jeered.

She shuddered. As she glanced at the magazine, she registered the fact that it held yesterday's date. So Zero couldn't have had it for long. "When did you get this?"

"This morning, after Finn left. So, no, I haven't told him yet. But don't think I won't," he warned.

In the absence of any better tactic, she decided to brave it out. "I don't know what you mean."

"Sure you do, sex kitten. What, was Finn getting close to figuring you out? So you, like, had to throw your body at him to keep him occupied?"

She shut her eyes against the ugly accusation. "You know it's not like that between Finn and me."

"Gimme a break, Angel," he said sourly. "Everybody saw you two last night. We all know what you were doing."

Angie took a deep breath. "Zero, you don't understand."

"Oh, yes, I do." Zero shoved one leather fist in her direction. "I understand all about you and your scummy boyfriend in Washington, and Finn's gonna know, too. If that tub of cop lard didn't already tell him, I will."

"No, you can't tell him." She tried to be soft and convincing. "Zero, you have to know how much that would hurt Finn. You don't want that, do you?"

"That's why I want you out of here." His eyes were dark and accusing. "You lied to him, and you hurt him, and Finn is my friend. I think maybe he even loves you." Unsteadily, he continued, "You get out of here, Angel, now, and I won't say anything. But if you don't haul your sex kitten butt off this farm in ten minutes, Finn's going to know the whole thing."

"I'm sorry, Zero." She put a gentle hand on his arm, holding it there even as he tried to snatch it away from her touch. "I'm sorry that it turned out this way."

"Will you shove off and leave us alone?"

"So if I agree to leave, you won't tell Finn?"

"That's the deal," he said sullenly.

Running away hadn't worked the first time, and it wasn't going to work this time, either. That much was clear. "Well, I'm sorry to disappoint you, Zero, but I'm not leaving."

She had only one chance to salvage something of her pride and her integrity. Finn might not understand, Zero certainly wouldn't understand, but Angie knew she'd made the right choice.

"I promised Finn I would stay," she said softly. She picked the magazine up off the table and offered it to Zero. "I promised."

He brandished it at her like a sword of truth. "Then he's gonna read all about you and Washington and everything you did. I warned you."

"I know." She swallowed. "I know you want me to go, because in your heart, you think that would be best for Finn. But I can't go, not before I tell him the truth."

"I don't believe you'll tell him," he taunted. "You'll just lie to him again."

"I won't—"

"You shoulda told him before you let him fall for you." Zero turned away and muttered to the back door, "He loves you."

"I love him, too." The words sounded heavy and important as they hung there in the stuffy kitchen, mocking her. So why was she telling Zero this? And why hadn't she realized it before now? "I love him," she said again. "And that's why he needs to hear this from me. Will you let me be the one to tell him?"

"Why did you have to come here and screw everything up?" he asked sorrowfully. "Finn never had any girlfriends before, and it was better. It was lots better."

"I didn't mean to—"

"Do you think it matters what you *mean?* You did it, you did all of it, and now you're gonna pay."

And then he dashed out the back door.

Angie stood in the middle of the kitchen, feeling a hundred years old. She hadn't even gotten used to the fact that she'd slept with Finn, fallen head over heels in love with the man of her dreams. Now it was all in ashes.

"I never had to deal with anything like this," she protested to the empty kitchen. "My family never yelled—ever. I was brought up to get along and keep quiet, not to shout at people or tell the truth."

She had no clue how to deal with Zero, let alone what to say to Finn when the time came. Should she go after the boy? Or should she wait for Finn? Which disaster was she supposed to tackle first?

"Oh, God." She sat down at the kitchen table and put her head in her hands. "I am totally unequipped to deal with this."

"With what?" he asked.

She turned. "Finn . . ." But the second she saw his face, she knew. "Oh, my God. You know, don't you?"

"What is it I'm supposed to know?"

"About me."

"You mean there's something you didn't tell me?" he asked sarcastically. "And what would that be? Maybe that the FBI is after you?" He pounded a fist onto the table so hard that the fruit bowl in the middle bounced up and down. "Or maybe that the mob is after you?" His arm shot out, sweeping the bowl off the table and rolling apples and oranges every which way.

"I didn't—"

"Or maybe that you slept with some sleaze-bucket politician who cheated the government out of a couple million?" he demanded, and his voice was so soft and deadly, she flinched from hearing it. "Or were you the one who did the stealing? Which one of the lovebirds hatched the plan?"

"Did Zero tell you this?"

"No. Mel Sibley got an APB that matched you. Angel-Angie—it wasn't hard once he'd seen you, even with the hair." He glanced over at her quickly. "Are you saying Zero knows? Oh, no, he's probably going to kill somebody."

"He's not going to kill anybody except me." She smiled bitterly. "Unless you do it first."

"I better go find him," he muttered. "He's liable to do just about anything."

"He told me he wouldn't tell you if I agreed to go far, far away."

"And?"

"And what?"

"And what did you tell him?" Finn's expression was so remote, she would've needed air transportation to reach him. "Are you going or staying?"

"Are you saying that staying is a possibility?"

"You tell me." He gave her a thin, humorless smile. "Is your pretty little bottom going to be in jail for a long, long time? It's tricky to milk a cow from the inside of the state pen, you know."

"Are you planning on turning me in?"

Finn shook his head and directed his gaze into the farthest corner of the kitchen, well away from Angie. "Why couldn't you tell me?" His gaze was etched with sorrow, brushed with pain, as it flickered back over her. "I just don't understand why you couldn't tell me."

"At first I was afraid that you would turn me in. And then..." She licked her lip. "And then I was afraid that I would lose you."

She wanted to put her arms around him; she wanted him to grab her and hug her and tell her it would all be okay. But as Angie waited in the quiet kitchen, neither of those possibilities came to pass.

"Finn," she ventured, "you said you'd always be on my side. Are you still on my side, even a little?"

"That was before I knew who you were sleeping with," he said roughly. "That was before I found out I was number who-knows-what in a series of patsies. Just one of the men used and betrayed by Angie Marie Boone on her independent voyage to big bucks. Sounds like a good one for TV."

"I'm not like that." His words flayed her like a whip. "I didn't steal anything, and I never slept with him."

"Then why do so many people think you did?"

"I don't care what any of them think," she returned heatedly. "Except you. You have to know I wouldn't do that—I wouldn't make love—with anyone but you."

"How do I know?" he challenged. "Because you told me so?"

"Because you know me. You've lived here with me." She grabbed his arm and made him look at her. "We fought, but there was always respect under that. There was still something between us that meant trust and understanding."

Finn said nothing, and she wanted to slap some sense into him.

"Why would I be hanging around here if I had all that money?" she demanded. "And why would I be alone if I had this rich, stupid boyfriend who went on the lam with me? Doesn't logic fly in the face of me ending up here, a charity case, if I was this Black Widow you seem to think I am?"

"So why didn't you stay and fight, if you were so innocent, if you didn't do anything wrong?"

"Because the deck was stacked against me!" She squeezed harder on his arm. "Why can't you believe me?"

"I don't know," he said coldly, shaking off her hand and taking refuge near the back door.

"Yes, you do," she argued. "Finn, think about it. You know me better than that."

"What I know is that you put me and the kids in very grave danger."

"I'm sorry about that."

"Great." His eyes were blazing with anger as his gaze swept her accusingly. "Your apology really doesn't take the sting out, you know? A gross of bullet-proof vests might be a better option." His laugh was short and hard. "Hell, for all we know, Al Capone and the gang are out there right now, getting ready to shoot holes in my kids!"

And that's when the shots rang out.

Chapter Thirteen

"What was that?" Angie demanded, hurrying to the back door. She opened it wide, scanning the snowy field between the house and the barn. "I don't see anything. A car backfiring, do you think?"

Quickly, Finn grabbed her and hauled her away from the door. "Cars don't usually backfire in the middle of a field."

Stealthily moving around her, he made his way to the back window and peered out around the edge of the curtain. He looked like an outlaw in a bad western, holed up in his hideout during the climactic shootout with the posse. Only this time, she was the outlaw, and that was no posse out there.

In fact, she wasn't quite sure *who* was out there. Bad guys? Good guys? Or maybe neither. Maybe this was all a coincidence of timing.

"A hunter?" she asked hopefully.

"No hunter would be shooting at my house," he snapped.

As if to punctuate his words, there was a loud crack from out back, and then a faint ping at the back door, right where Angie had been standing. As she watched, horrified, the windowpane ten feet in front of her simply exploded into a million pieces. Cold air blasted into the kitchen through the gaping hole.

"Get down!" Finn ordered, but Angie just stood there like a statue, gazing mutely at the shards of glass littering the floor in front of her feet.

There was blood on her face. She could feel the wetness trickling down her cheek. Was it from shattering glass, or had she been grazed by whatever it was that came through the door?

She couldn't move, couldn't think, couldn't breathe. "The door," she said woodenly. "They broke the glass in the door."

"Angel, get down. Now!" he commanded, but she still didn't move. Swearing, Finn threw himself at her, shoving her away from the glass, tackling her and shielding her from stray bullets with his long, hard body.

All she said was "Oof" as she hit the deck facedown. There were two more hard blasts of sound from out back, echoing in the still morning air, followed by an odd, buzzing, ricochet noise. Angie felt as if she had fallen into a slow-motion video. She couldn't catch her breath trapped under him this way. She couldn't even raise her head.

"Finn?" she tried, shifting around. But he was heavy above her, ramming her into the bottom of the kitchen cabinets on the other side. She was protected from the bullets, but she was also scared to death. And there was blood dripping into her eye, burning and blinding her. A splinter of glass had pierced through her jeans near her hip, and every time she moved even a tiny bit, it embedded itself farther into her skin.

"Lie still," he said impatiently. "The shots seem to be coming from behind the chicken coop. We have to stay as far out of the line of the door as we can."

"Shots?"

"Shots," he repeated. "What did you think it was? Bows and arrows?"

"I—I can't believe someone's shooting at us."

"Believe it," he said tersely.

"Hey!" a man shouted from the same direction the shots had come. It was a vicious, ugly sound, full of contempt and bravado, thundering out across the clearing and into the kitchen, wrapping around her and squeezing the life out of her. Angie closed her eyes against the sound. "We know she's in there," the man bellowed. "Hand over the broad and the dough and nobody gets hurt!"

Immediately, Finn's hand swept up to cover her mouth. "Don't say anything," he cautioned in her ear. "They want you to yell back so they'll know where you are. So whatever you do, whatever you say, make it quiet, okay?"

Silent, she nodded.

"How many of them do you think there are?" he asked.

"I don't know," she whispered back. "I don't even know who they are."

Briskly, he spoke into her ear. "I'm guessing one or two from the sound of the shots. Maybe three, if one's posted out front to watch the door. Thank God they're not using a machine gun, or we'd both be splattered from here to kingdom come."

"Why did they stop shooting all of a sudden?"

"To move closer, I think. Which means we've got to get out of here," he told her. "We're sitting ducks this way. All they have to do is keep shooting and keep moving in closer, and there's not a damn thing we can do."

She wanted to roll over and hang on to Finn, to let him carry her out of here, away from danger. But this was only Finn's problem by proxy. She was the one who'd brought trouble to Heavenly Acres, and now it should be her responsibility to put an end to it. But how?

With a lull in the shooting, she could hear the calm tick-tock of the kitchen clock above the sink. Ticktock, tick-tock, as the seconds of her life passed away and some crazy lunatic took potshots at the back door.

"I think we can make a run for it out the side door," Finn mused. "They probably don't know there's another door, since it's pretty well hidden, and they can't see that side of the house from where they are. Once we're out, it's a straight shot to the boys' bunkhouse, if we run like hell across the side yard. No cover except a couple of trees, but we should be okay as long as the bad guys stay where they are. I don't know if you're religious, Angel, but you better start praying that there's only two of them, and that they're not moving around too much."

"I'm praying," she whispered.

"Good. All right then, let's decide how we're going to get out of here in one piece."

"Look, Finn, you can't do this." She crawled out from under him and braced herself against the cabinet door. Wearily, she announced, "It's me they want. So I'm just going to walk out the back door and let them take me. It will solve everything."

"Do you really think I'd let you do that?" he asked fiercely.

"It's the only way." Angie's voice was bleak. "Even if we could make it, we can't run to the bunkhouse. That's where all the kids are. Do you think I would lead a bunch of murderers straight to the kids?"

He leaned over closer, skimming his knuckles against her cheek. His hand came away streaked with scarlet. "If you won't come willingly," he said quietly, in a voice so dangerous it should have come with a warning label, "I swear I'll pick you up and drag you to the bunkhouse myself."

"No," she persisted, but Finn clenched his jaw and reached for her. "No," she said again, shrugging him off.

His fingers tightened around her wrist. "Angie, we're going to get out of here. You and me."

"But the children . . ."

Finn eased in closer, sliding his arms around her, resting his forehead on hers for a long pause. "We haven't got time to argue about it. Once we get to the bunkhouse, we'll safeguard the kids first, before we do anything else. But I'm not leaving you here."

"I could—"

"No," he said flatly.

She hesitated, but she knew she was just wasting time by being stubborn. There was no getting around Finn on this one. "Okay," she said softly.

"All right. Here's what we do," he said intently. "Crawl over to the side door, you first. Without a sound, not one peep, we slide open the door to the porch, and then we sneak down to the yard. Once you hit the ground, you run as fast as you can, okay? No looking back to see where I am or where they are—just haul your tail like you've got afterburners."

"The cat," she reminded him.

"What about her?"

"She's in the house somewhere. If those gangsters come blasting into the house, she might get in the way." Angie was adamant. "I'm not leaving the cat."

"Okay." He took a deep breath and kissed her full on the lips. "I'll get the cat. You get out of here. Now!"

Scooting along like a sand crab, Angie pushed open the door with one hand and streaked out to the porch and freedom. Her feet hit hard, crunchy snow, and she winced at the noise, but she kept going. Too bad she'd never taken up jogging as a hobby. She could've used a little practice about now.

And then she was halfway across the yard, almost to the cover of a clump of trees. Where was Finn? He should be right behind her, but she couldn't feel him, couldn't hear him. She was puffing and choking in the cold air as she raced behind the trunk of a winter-bare apple tree. Clutching her side, almost doubling over, she watched for Finn.

Where the hell was he?

"He's got to be okay," she whispered. "No more shots, and I didn't hear him fall. Maybe he had trouble finding the cat. But it shouldn't take this long. Where is he?"

And then someone grabbed her from behind.

"What are you doing?" he demanded. The cat was dangling over one of his arms, and she didn't look pleased. A low, rumbling growl emanated from Gribble.

Angie's heart was still pounding as she collapsed into his arms, hugging him and the cat. "Thank God you're okay."

"Me?"

"You weren't behind me—I didn't know where you disappeared to."

"I'm just quieter than you are," he grumbled. "I thought I told you to get your butt to the bunkhouse and not look back."

Angie composed herself, disengaging herself and glaring at him. "What about you? If you'd gotten your butt to the bunkhouse without looking back, you wouldn't have known I stopped."

"You were huffing and puffing like an old lady," he muttered. "I was afraid you'd passed out or something."

"I'm fine," she insisted.

"Then we better get going."

He cast a worried glance around them, but there was only the eerie silence of the winter wind rushing through the trees. No more gunfire, no more whistling bullets. Catching her arm and hoisting Gribble into a more secure position, he guided them through the trees and, finally, around to the back door of the boys' bunkhouse.

Immediately, they were surrounded by a cluster of boys and girls. "What's going on? What were those noises?" they chorused, pressing close.

"Nothing to worry about," Finn assured them. He dumped the cat on the floor, and it immediately shot away to seek shelter under a bed. "Everybody needs to stay calm, okay? There are some bad people out there looking for Angel, and we need to make sure everybody plays it safe."

"Angel?" one of the younger boys squeaked. "Why do they want Angel?"

"It doesn't matter, okay?" Finn surveyed the room quickly. "Angel, will you take these kids upstairs and count them? I'm going to go check out the girls' bunkhouse and make sure we've got them all in one place. I want everybody accounted for, and then we'll plot some strategy."

There wasn't time to argue, so she herded a gaggle of excited children up the stairs and into the large dormitory-style room where the boys slept. She counted heads, trying desperately to remember how many there should be. With a little help, she made up a list and checked off names. After accounting for the stragglers from the other bunkhouse, they had all but two.

"Layla and Derek," she said with rising fear. "I haven't seen them this morning. I thought they'd be over here."

"No," the other kids countered. "We haven't seen them, either."

"I know they weren't in the house." Angie clasped her hands firmly, trying not to show how worried she was. "Do you think they could be in the woodworking shop or somewhere?"

"I'm sure they're safe," Finn returned quickly. "We have to assume they holed up when they first heard the shots, just like everyone else did. We'll find them when this is all over, and I'm sure they'll be fine."

Angie was left to help out as best she could, soothing nerves and damping down panic, as Finn took charge around her. Swiftly, he assigned a couple of the older girls to watch the rest, with special instructions to make sure no one wandered outside. Then he commandeered Zero, and the two of them trooped back downstairs. Determined to be in on whatever it was they were plotting, Angie followed.

"Why do you think we haven't heard any more shooting?" she asked quietly.

Finn's gaze flashed to hers. "My guess is they're searching the house, looking for us." He shrugged. "Takes a long time to look in all those closets, go through every nook and cranny in the basement."

"So we're safe for a little while?"

"Until they figure out we escaped, and they see our footprints in the snow leading right here."

She paled. "We can't let them come here. The kids..."

"I know." He grimaced. "That's why we need to come up with a plan. What do you say, Zero? Are you in?"

Giving Angie the benefit of his sulkiest attitude, Zero mumbled that he wasn't saying anything while she was in the room, but Finn waved that away with an impatient hand. "We haven't got time for arguments, Zero. You want to help out or not?"

"Not with no sex kitten," the boy said contemptuously.

"Zero, this isn't the time, okay? You're the best brain I have to find a way out of this mess." Finn set an arm around his young friend's shoulders. "Help me, Z."

Zero straightened his shoulders awkwardly, obviously proud to be chosen as Finn's second-in-command. "Yeah, okay. Y'know, Finn, with me and you on it, those guys don't stand a chance."

"So, what do you think?"

"Well, we could distract 'em, like with a big noise," Zero said eagerly. "And then when we had 'em in one place, we could ambush 'em, maybe, and run 'em over with the tractor."

"They'd have to stand still and let you do it," Angie commented dryly.

"Okay, so what's your plan?" Zero asked with a scowl.

"My plan is to get me off this farm however we can. As soon as I'm gone, they'll go, because they'll try to follow me."

Zero nodded reluctantly. "She's right, Finn. We gotta get her a way out."

"I agree."

Angie glanced over, shocked. He agreed with her?

"But if you get in the truck and start driving, they'll be after you like a shot." He held his jaw so firmly that she could hear his teeth grind. "They'll find you wherever you head, Angel, and it won't be pretty when they do. I'm not throwing you to the wolves.''

I'm not throwing you to the wolves. It almost sounded as if he still cared. *Don't get your hopes up,* she told herself. Even if he were madly in love, she'd still be facing death and dismemberment from whoever was out there, firing off rounds from the henhouse. Any future with Finn was going to be very short-lived if she didn't deal with the hoodlums first.

"So," Zero interjected, "what do we do?"

"A three-pronged attack," Finn returned. "There are three of us, so we each take a part."

Obviously, he'd already thought out what he wanted them to do, and he was only playing around pretending to listen to their suggestions so they'd feel a part of the effort. But Angie was not sure she could agree. *We each take a part,* he'd said, which meant he was expecting Zero to take on a job, too.

"No, Finn. It's not right." Angie put a hand on Finn's arm. "Zero is a child, and there's no way I'm going to countenance risking his safety on my account."

"Hey, I can do my part just fine!"

"You already risked his safety, Angel, his and everybody else's." Finn turned away from her touch. "Zero's the best man for the job."

"Yeah!" the kid said toughly.

"Zero, do you have any more of those cherry bombs, the ones you blew up the johns with at Halloween?"

"Yeah," he said warily. "And some bottle rockets, too."

"Great. Go get them, will you?"

As Zero ran back and forth to his stash of fireworks, Angie asked, "What are you going to do with those?"

"A diversion," Finn replied, as he stuffed his pockets full of explosives. "I think Zero's right, we need a diversion, something to pull those guys as far away as possible from the bunkhouses and also from what else we're trying to pull off. So that'll be me."

"The diversion?" Angie swallowed around a lump in her throat. "You're going to distract them so they'll come after you?"

"That's about the size of it." He checked his pockets for matches, and then sent Zero for something to stick the rockets in.

"Finn, I can't let you do this. That's too dangerous."

"It's done," he said flatly, taking three or four empty cans as the boy handed them over. "Zero, your part is pretty easy. Run. Run like you're going for an Olympic medal. It's about two miles to the Johnsons' farm, and I want you to call the sheriff as soon as you get there."

"Aw, Finn, that's no fun," he groused. "Why can't I do the cherry bombs?"

"Because you're the fastest runner." Finn let a note of frustration slip into his voice. "I know it's really dangerous, and if there was any other way, I'd do it myself. But Zero, you're our only shot at getting to a phone."

"Well, okay..."

"All right then. Take off the back way."

Angie wasn't fooled. Finn had just given Zero a fairly safe task, as tasks went at the moment, but he'd purposely made it sound more perilous. Meanwhile, he'd saved the most hazardous job for himself. And Angie was worried.

"When you set off this stuff, won't they come after you?"

"That's the whole idea."

"Finn, please don't," she pleaded. "Now that Zero's gone for the authorities, I can just drive away the other direction. I'll be okay."

Giving no indication he'd heard, Finn strode for the door. "As soon as you hear the first cherry bomb go off, go around through the trees to the barn. That's where I parked the truck." He tossed her the keys. "If they left their own car in the driveway, drive around it, but I doubt they did."

"Finn, are you listening to me?"

"No." He glanced over at her briefly. "What you want just doesn't matter anymore. I have to keep my kids safe, so I have to keep those guys going the wrong direction."

"But they may shoot you!"

"They're not going to shoot me."

She shook her head, wanting nothing more than to grab him and keep him safe in the bunkhouse. "I don't think you were born to be a diversion, Finn."

"Well, that's not my only function. I'm also going to scout around for Derek and Layla, and hope I fall over them before those clowns with the guns do." A bitter smile curved his narrow lips. "I guess you got the idea I was doing this for you. As usual, Angel, you're wrong.''

"You sound like the prosecutor, judge and jury all rolled into one," she said slowly. "Do you remember telling me that no matter what I did, you wouldn't judge me?"

His eyes were as cold as the winter wind howling through the trees. "That was before you brought the mob to my farm."

And then he ducked out the front door, pockets bulging with penny-ante firecrackers, matches and empty pop cans for missile silos.

"They're shooting with guns, and he's got bottle rockets," she whispered. "Oh, Finn, what have I done to you?"

But even as she said the words, she heard a loud boom shake the earth and rattle the trees, and she knew that Finn had set off a cherry bomb on the other side of the clearing.

"My turn," she murmured, hoping she was up to the challenge. At the moment, getting away from the farm sounded wonderful.

With adrenaline churning through her system, she skirted around the outbuildings on her way to the back of the barn. Several times, she thought she heard signs of the intruders, but once it was only the whistle and pop of a bottle rocket, sent up by Finn from who-knew-where, and another time it was a broken branch, blown across her path. Angie tried to calm her nerves, but she had never been so scared in all her life.

Cautiously, she plastered herself to the side of the barn, looking every which way for bad guys. But there was nothing.

Boom! She jumped where she stood, and had to stick a hand over her mouth to keep from crying out.

Finn had tossed a cherry bomb way over beyond the alfalfa field, judging from the cloud of snow and dirt kicked up in that direction. He was certainly covering some ground, she'd say that for him. And every time she heard one of his explosions, she knew he was still okay.

"Hey, JoJo!" somebody yelled in a gruff, guttural voice. "Way over there. See that?"

She jammed herself back up against the barn. It was them! As she hid there, making herself as small as possible, two men, both burly, both dressed in dark suits, raced out of a grove of nearby trees and took off across a snow-covered field, heading toward Finn and the cherry bomb.

"Over there!" shouted the shorter one, the one called JoJo. Way out in front of him, he had a squared-off silver gun, and the barrel glinted dully in the pale morning light, sending chills up Angie's spine. "What the hell are they doing?" JoJo howled. "These clowns are for the birds!"

He and his partner kept on running, tripping and sliding on the slippery ground, their guns out-stretched, until she was sure one of them would fall and kill himself. JoJo especially was so short and squat, she couldn't figure out how he managed to cover any distance. But he was pretty quick for a stubby, chubby little guy.

When she decided they were far enough away not to be an immediate danger, she slid around the barn the other way and sneaked inside.

Finn's truck gleamed softly, invitingly, in the dim barn, as if it were waiting just for her. Relief filled her as she climbed into the driver's seat and inserted the keys. *Home free now,* she thought. She would drive away like the Pied Piper of Hamelin, dragging the rats along with her, and Finn and the children would be safe.

And maybe, just maybe, the cops would find her in time to keep the thugs from rubbing her out.

Chug, chug, chug. The engine wouldn't quite catch. She pumped the accelerator and tried again. But chug, chug, chug was all she got.

How much noise was she making? Why wouldn't the lousy pickup start?

Chug, chug, chug.

"What am I doing wrong?" she cried in frustration, pounding her hands on the wheel.

Chug, chug, chug. And then a snap. A snap that didn't belong.

Feeling like a mouse caught in a trap, Angie lifted her eyes.

"Lookee what I got," JoJo said. He was holding his big, cold, silver gun pointed right at her head as he eased open her door. "I got me one runaway broad."

Chapter Fourteen

Immediately, she lifted her hands skyward, in the universal gesture of surrender she'd seen in a million bad movies. The two gorillas backed up, waving her out of the pickup, and she descended as gingerly as she could.

Trying hard to maintain a sense of composure, she said carefully, "Look, I don't have a weapon or anything. So there's no reason to get jumpy and do anything we'd both regret. We'll just stay nice and calm and friendly, okay?"

"Shaddup," JoJo snapped.

So much for rapprochement. The burly little gangster's gun was trained precisely at her right temple, and she stilled, trying to get her heartbeat into a less terrified rhythm, desperate to avoid any moves this sort of thug might interpret as suspicious.

She peered at him more closely, curious despite her fear. She'd never actually seen a mobster before. This one, this JoJo person, who was only about as tall as she was, but at least three times as wide. And he appeared to have no neck, no neck at all. How did somebody get to look like that?

"So, doll, where's the cash?" he growled.

"I, uh, don't have any money. I never did," she swore.

"Mr. Anthony don't like jokes, doll." He shook his massive head, and she saw a funny gleam in his beady eyes. "Mr. Anthony wants his money."

"But I don't have it."

He raised his gun again, and smiled. Or at least it looked like he was trying to smile. His piggy little eyes almost completely disappeared, and his chin dipped even lower into the place where his neck should've been.

"You ain't gonna be alive long enough to tell me that again, broad."

She really hated being called a broad. "I don't have any money!" she retorted, forgetting she was supposed to be temperate and smart. She'd had the worst day of her life, and she didn't care if this little hoodlum was the Godfather and the Terminator rolled into one unattractive package. He was a lowlife blockhead, and she was very impatient. "Go tell your Mr. Anthony he got the wrong person, okay? I'm really sorry, but it's that scumbucket Lance Hocker he should be threatening, not me!"

A low roar started to emanate from JoJo, and he lumbered closer, clutching his gun and pointing it, then roaring again and flexing his other fist, as if he couldn't quite decide whether he wanted to strangle her or shoot her first. His pal, the taller, not quite so hefty thug, advanced on her, too, doing his best to look as menacing as JoJo.

"The broad's got a death wish," JoJo snarled. "I say we give her what she wants."

"Yeah," his pal snarled along with him, and Angie squeezed her eyes shut before she had to watch either of them pull the trigger.

Instead, she heard a strange whooshing noise, followed by the most godawful smell.

"It smells like..." She opened one eye. "Manure."

It was manure all right, mixed with hay and straw and regular old garbage from the smell of it, and JoJo and his pal were buried in it. She could hear them thrashing around and trying to talk underneath the pile. But manure was slippery stuff, and they couldn't seem to get a foothold.

A laugh escaped her, and then another. Catching a glint of silver near the edge of this jolly little compost heap, she stooped and examined it. "Lookee what I found," she said, echoing JoJo. Delicately, she removed JoJo's gun from where it had apparently fallen when he got hit by the avalanche of muck.

"How in the world did this happen?" she asked out loud.

"Us!" a tiny voice piped up from the back of a hayrack parked nearby.

"Derek?"

"Me, too," Layla chimed in, joining her brother at the back of the wagon. "We dumped a whole load on 'em."

"We both had to push to get it to go," Derek added with importance.

He scampered down from the hayrack, and she scooped him up for a heartfelt hug. Luckily, he didn't smell anywhere near as awful as the refuse heap he'd been playing with.

"They were bad, Angel," he said solemnly. "They yelled at you and they were very bad."

"I know." Angie pressed close to Derek, trying not to think about what a close call she'd just had. Brightening, she put on a smile and surveyed this hayrack miracle. "What was a wagonload of garbage doing sitting there, and how did you guys lower the boom with it?"

"Dunno." Joining them down by the truck, Layla shrugged her thin shoulders. "Dunno the first part, I mean. We just made the back part go down and it fell right out for the second part." She shrugged again. Angie couldn't figure out what the heck she was talking about, but she wasn't about to argue with such timely intervention.

"Zero's been collecting icky stuff for a while, up on the hayrack," Layla went on after a moment of consideration. "He wanted to be stable-mucker every day for a whole week, and he got a lot, didn't he?"

"Yes, he did," Angie said politely. She was trying not to laugh, but this had to be the most bizarre way on record to catch criminals.

"I think it was for a joke or something," Layla chattered on. "It was like, oh, I dunno, I forget the word. But they did it in *Robin Hood,* where you put something on one side of like a slide, and then jump real hard on the other side, and then, kaplooey, it flies through the air. But we didn't jump.''

''I think you mean a catapult.'' Well, that fit. Zero was probably planning to launch manure at her if she didn't leave the farm. He was very fond of bad-smelling jokes. ''I still don't know how you did it, but I guess it doesn't matter. You guys were wonderful,'' she told him, gathering them close. ''Better than Robin Hood.''

''Looks like you got the bad guys, Angel, all by yourself.''

Finn. She stiffened, holding her ground with the children. His voice gave away no emotion, no clue as to whether he was still angry, or relieved and happy now that the danger to the farm was past. ''Actually, I had lots of help,'' she said slowly. She rose from the ground, still holding Derek close, with her other hand in Layla's.

She turned, not sure she was ready to face him yet, but taking her chances. ''What's the verdict, Finn?''

''Verdict?''

From the closed expression on his chiseled features, she wasn't sure there was a verdict. And he had no opportunity to say more, because suddenly a dark sedan came crashing into the barn behind him, nearly rear-ending the truck.

First a load of men in dark suits spilled out of the car, and then another bunch came rushing in from outside. They were all shouting ''FBI'' and flashing their credentials every which way. One or more of them started to poke at the pile of manure, uncovering the two hoods and carting them off in all their foul-smelling glory.

And then there were sirens and police cars and Zero, with a new set of authorities also shouting and running around, wanting statements and quotes and asking questions. Finally, somebody or other figured out that Angie was the source of all this mayhem, that she was none other than America's Most Wanted, Angie Marie Boone. That was when the hubbub really kicked into high gear.

Finn took Derek out of her arms as the little boy cried out, "Angel? Where are they taking you?"

But the FBI agents were already reading her her rights and handcuffing her and leading her away. One of them pulled too quickly, and she stumbled, clumsy without her hands for balance.

"Damn it, you don't have to hurt her," Finn said savagely. He shoved away the agent who'd caused the problem.

"Hey, mister, lay off," the guy shouted. "You want us to arrest you, too?"

"Finn, please, don't make it any worse than it already is." Angie fell against him, closing her eyes and taking what might be her last chance to feel protected inside the hard circle of his arms. He held her tightly, so tightly she couldn't breathe. "It's okay," she told him, disentangling herself as the agent nudged her away.

"No, it's not," he said roughly.

But she had no choice. Her guards led her to the car, opening the back door and motioning her inside.

"Finn?" she called out. "Finn, I love you." It wasn't loud, but she knew he heard. Everybody standing around heard, too, but she didn't care. Quietly, she said, "I didn't get a chance to tell you that before, and I wanted you to know. I love you."

He nodded, but then the door slammed shut, and Angie rode away in silence to meet her uncertain, unwelcome fate.

THE TELEVISION WAS ON in the prison visitors' room, providing a comforting blur and some voices in the background. Alone, waiting, Angie pretended she was watching the end of a soap.

Around her, about a half-dozen prisoners, dressed in faded blue jumpsuits just like hers, chatted with their visitors. One pretty young woman was crying as she rocked her baby in her arms, while another, tougher customer was in a lip-lock with her boyfriend over in the corner. There were all kinds in this place, and Angie was now just one of the bunch.

Model Prisoner U.S.A. It wasn't exactly what she'd envisioned as a career goal.

Whoever it was who wanted to talk to her hadn't arrived yet, and she was trying to figure out who it would be this time. So far, in her eight-and-a-half days inside the correctional facility, her visitors had not been inspiring.

She'd had quite a few members of the law enforcement community, all trying to threaten her or sweet-talk her into telling them where Lance and the money had disappeared to.

"I don't know" was all she could really say. Her lawyer, a cute and very young man sent over by Gretchen, had instructed her not to say anything at all, but she disobeyed him flagrantly, spilling everything she knew to anyone who asked. After all, how much could "I don't know" hurt her?

Then there were the members of the press. They told her they wanted to delve into whatever it was in her childhood that made her turn to a life of crime. Even better, they were hoping for some steamy sex scandal, with her and Lance in *flagrante delicto* for all of America to see.

If only they knew how boring her story really was. Oh, yeah, she'd keep America glued to the TV, all right: inept government worker who never stole anything more expensive than a twenty-nine-cent stamp, who didn't sleep with her boss and didn't betray anybody, runs for her life and makes a fool of herself in the process.

The plain truth was, the only interesting or exciting thing that had happened to her was falling in love with Finn, and nobody was going to want to hear about that. Especially since there was no happy ending.

Angie slumped farther down in her uncomfortable plastic chair. Yeah, her life was a real peach right about now.

Aside from cops and reporters, her visitors were sparse. She'd talked to her mother on the telephone, but the elder Boones were having a hard time understanding what had happened. Political scandal wasn't exactly part of their world. She was glad, in a way, not to have to face them. They'd been so sure her life in the big city would corrupt her, and even if it hadn't, she was in no mood for "I told you so."

Gretchen had made an appearance, weeping buckets as she told Angie how very sorry she was that Jake Gannon, federal agent, had turned out to be a two-timing, office-bugging snake. Actually, as Gretchen admitted later in the conversation, she and Jake were still seeing each other, since he'd groveled and told her he felt just terrible about the bug *and* the late arrival at the farm, after JoJo "the Mongoose" Mando and the other thug had almost killed her.

No hard feelings, Angie assured her friend.

Her only other interesting caller was none other than the mysterious Mr. Anthony, employer of JoJo "the Mongoose" Mando. From her various conversations with the FBI, Angie now knew Mr. Anthony to be a reputed mobster called the Elevator Man. She had even heard the story of his moniker, making her thank her lucky stars there were no elevators at Heavenly Acres Farm.

As it turned out, the Elevator Man was a very shrewd old bugger. All he did was sit there in the visitors' room staring at her for about five minutes, after which he picked up his overcoat and his hat and shook his head.

"It ain't you," he spit out with disgust. "So Hocker suckered me out of my money and suckered us all into thinking it was you who done it, huh?"

"I guess so," she replied as kindly as she could. After all, there *were* elevators at the federal women's prison, so Angie preferred not to antagonize Mr. Anthony. She added, "I really don't know anything about it one way or the other."

"Ahh, this burns me," he groused. "This really burns me. The wrong dame, no money—how can a man do business this way?"

And then he left as quietly as he'd arrived. Since he'd called her "the wrong dame," she felt she could now safely assume she was off the hook with the mob, if not with the federal authorities.

From the frequency and length of visits from her pals at the FBI, she knew they still didn't believe her story of complete innocence. New charges were being added every day, according to her lawyer, and the FBI continued to question her about her role at the DHA, her relationship with Lance, and what she was doing during every minute of her entire stay at Heavenly Acres.

She was numb with answering their stupid questions.

She told them most of it, painting wickedly descriptive pictures of Lance and Bibi, but she danced around the part about Finn. It was too fresh and too painful still, and she just didn't think it was any of their business.

"So who will it be today?" she pondered. "The cute one, the fat one, the mean one, or the one who keeps popping antacids?" By now, she knew her FBI agents by heart.

On the far wall, a very attractive couple on the soap started to get amorous, casting smoky glances at each other, saying naughty things, and Angie's eyes fastened on it against her will. The man was dark, with a

gorgeous chest, and he reminded her much too much
of someone she didn't want to be reminded of.

Her mind put Finn's face on the TV actor, and she
felt the stirrings of a familiar hunger. If only she could
touch him, trace that little scar in his eyebrow one
more time. . . .

She would've been content, she told herself, not
even to touch, but just to drink him in with her eyes,
to gaze her fill. If only she could so embed him in her
mind that he would still be with her when she rolled
into her awful bunk in this horrible place.

"It's been too long," she whispered.

"Too long since what?"

She shot up in her plastic chair, almost knocking the
clumsy thing over completely. With her cheeks burning, she stood up and spun around. It was like calling
up a genie out of a bottle. She wanted him and presto,
there he was, as big as life, as glowing and vital and
drop-dead, knock-down-drag-out spectacular as he'd
ever been.

Tight jeans, black T-shirt, leather jacket . . . Those
shoulders, that Rebel Without a Cause face . . . It was
enough to make her swoon and scream and beat him
with her fists, all in the same moment.

"What are you doing here?" she demanded. She
ached to be in his arms, but she had no right to seek
shelter there. Hugging herself tightly, she took a ragged breath. "I have to say, I'm very surprised to see
you."

He raised an eyebrow. "Who were you expecting?"

"Not you."

She sat back down, wiping sweaty palms against the fabric of her hideous jumpsuit. If she'd harbored any foolish desire that he would haul her into his arms and tell her what she wanted to hear—*I was a fool. I can't live without you*—the cool expression on his beautiful face burst that bubble in a matter of seconds.

"So why are you here, Finn?" she asked. She kicked a scuffed tennis shoe into the institutional green linoleum floor. "Is this gloating time, payback time, or just a lark?"

He said nothing.

"We both know you don't take vacations and you don't leave Heavenly Acres," she remarked, retreating into sarcasm as her best defense against wanting him so much. "So it must be pretty important for you to come all this way. Maybe you're feeling a little guilty," she suggested. "After all, St. Finn the Altruistic can't handle knowing there's somebody out there he didn't save. So let's patch it up, is that it?"

She stuck out a hand, amazed at her own bravado. But pressure was welling up behind her eyes, and she wanted him out of there before she burst into tears or something equally pitiful.

She kept her voice light and unconcerned. "We can still be friends, something like that?"

"No," he returned. He knelt down on the linoleum, savagely grabbing her flimsy chair and whipping it around. Now she was trapped by his arms and his hard, angry body. Staring into her eyes, Finn declared, "We can't be friends."

The tears were hovering there, in the periphery of her vision. "Okay, so you don't want to be friends," she said quickly, rambling on before the storm broke. "I mean, what do I care? I'm probably going to be serving ten to fifteen years in the federal pen, so what good would some meaningless friendship with you do me, anyway? So why don't you yell at me or whatever you had in mind, get it all off your chest, and then just go, okay?"

Desperate to retain some small measure of dignity, she squeezed her eyes shut against the hot tears. Her voice was very small when she said again, "Just go, okay?"

"Angel, I love you."

She kept her eyes shut.

"Angie," he tried again. His fingers brushed her cheek. "Could you open your eyes and look at me, please? I'm dying here."

"Did you say...?"

"Yes, I did." There was a funny, vulnerable smile playing over his lips as he sat back, waiting for her reaction. Finally, he reached for her, enveloping her in a stranglehold and lifting her completely off the floor. "I'm so sorry," he whispered. "I wanted to come in here like this knight in shining armor and make it all perfect, but..."

He shook his head, tightening his hold until she couldn't breathe. She didn't care.

"I never did this before, Angel. I never told anyone I loved them before."

Her heart turned over and her tears overflowed. "Lousy timing," she mumbled, trying to swipe at them with one hand and still hold on to Finn. "I can't believe you said that. I can't believe you love me." She started to laugh through the downpour. "I can't believe you left them all alone on the farm to come see me."

"I left right after you did." He pulled her back down into the chair, setting her securely on his lap and cradling her close for a long moment. "I got Floyd and his wife to stay at the farm—Floyd's married, did you know that? I didn't."

He was jumping around so much, he was starting to sound like her. Leaning over, he kissed her quickly, greedily, as if he needed reinforcement before he finished up.

"So Floyd and his wife are taking care of the kids. I went to see your parents," he said softly. "I needed to know if the other things you told me were true."

"My parents? Why on earth would you do that?"

"I thought maybe they'd want to help, get you a good lawyer and that kind of thing." He shook his head. "They didn't seem to understand."

"Salt of the earth," she said slowly. "But salt's not a whole lot to live on."

"And after your parents were sort of a bust, believe it or not—" he grinned "—I went to see my parents."

"Oh, my." She searched his features for clues. "Was it awful? You hate them! Why did you do that?"

"The money." His embrace loosened a bit, as he propped his chin on top of her head, and she felt the warm comfort of his breath against her hair. "I needed the money to get a really good lawyer, and to bail you out."

"Oh, Finn." Quietly, she offered, "I'm sorry. They were awful, weren't they?"

"It's not your fault." Raking a hand through his hair, Finn gazed at her with exasperation. "Yes, they were awful, but my brother wasn't so bad. Welles gave me the money. It's my trust fund, anyway, but Welles is the administrator. And he okayed the big bucks, enough to get you out of this damn place with plenty left over for better times ahead."

"I can't believe this."

"Believe it." He kissed her again, longer and deeper this time. "You were right. I do need a life, a whole life, more than just the farm and the kids."

"More? Like what?"

"Like you." His blue eyes were troubled as his gaze sought hers. "I want you to marry me—live with me on the farm. I know you want more from your life than the farm, and that's okay. Whatever you want, as long as we can be together. What do you think?"

Curling her arms around his neck, she smiled. "I think we can work something out."

"Is that a yes?"

As she prepared her answer, someone turned up the volume on the television in the background, and its insistent voices reminded her of her surroundings, bringing her back to an unpleasant reality.

Angie rested her forehead against his, blocking out the sounds. "I can't marry you if I'm in jail for the rest of my life," she whispered. "I can't even think about it with all of this hanging over my head."

"We'll fight it, and we'll win," he promised.

"I knew all along!" a loud voice cried from the TV.

Impatient, Finn released her, standing up and heading for the television set to turn it down.

"Wait," she told him. "I know that lady."

"The old lady on TV?"

"Yes." Angie wandered closer, trying to place the face. "From the train. She was the old grandma on the train from D.C. to Chicago, the one who said she was psychic."

"I had it a teensy bit muddled," the grandma shouted into the camera. "I thought it was Cuba, but it was Aruba." She giggled. "But I knew she was there somewhere."

"But she thought *I* was in Cuba," Angie murmured. "What is this all about?"

A reporter's face now filled the screen as he announced, in his heavily modulated voice, "There has been an astounding development in the DHA-sex-and-money scandal. Federal agents, acting on a tip from the psychic you just heard, appear to have located missing politician Lance Hocker early this morning. They report that Hocker was holed up in a villa in Aruba with a darling of the jet set."

This was interrupted by footage of Lance and Bibi, hiding their faces as they were dragged along by a gaggle of severe-looking agents.

Looking at Lance, Finn muttered, "I'm not worried anymore about what was between you and him. You'd never go for a creep like that."

Angie glanced over at him with love in her heart. Trust Finn to come up with something that dopey at a time like this.

"Hocker's companion, the Contessa Bibi von Kronenburg, has now been implicated in Hocker's allegedly criminal activities," the reporter droned on. "Both will be extradited back to the U.S. to face charges."

Finn's face was a study in confusion. "Bibi von Kronenburg? That was the name on that goofball passport you had. How in the hell did you get her IDs?"

"How did you know I had her IDs?"

He shrugged. "I searched your stuff."

"Finn! That was highly unethical of you."

"Does it really matter?" A wicked smile curved his lips. "You're free, Angie, free as a bird. This clears you, sweetheart."

In all the confusion, she hadn't gotten that far. "Do you really think so?"

Meanwhile, the reporter was still talking. "A highly placed source at the Office of the United States Attorney indicates that Angie Marie Boone, long thought to be Hocker's accomplice, is likely to be exonerated by these new developments. Boone is still in custody, but her release may be imminent, according to our source."

"It's incredible," she whispered. "Finn, tell me I'm not dreaming."

"You're not dreaming." He picked her up and kissed her, practically tossing her in the air with his exuberance.

"It's incredible," she said again. "But then, what hasn't been completely off-the-wall incredible since the first time I set my eyes on you in the train station in Champaign, Illinois?''

"Angie, do you know what this means?''

"I get to come home?''

"You get to come home.'' He held her close for a long moment. "And it looks like I get to keep my Angel.''

But she shook her head. "You ought to know by now, Finn—I'm no angel.''

"That's okay,'' he told her, with a reckless, wicked smile that took her breath away. "Neither am I.''

ROMANCE IS A YEARLONG EVENT!

Celebrate the most romantic day of the year with MY VALENTINE! (February)

CRYSTAL CREEK
When you come for a visit Texas-style, you won't want to leave! (March)

Celebrate the joy, excitement and adjustment that comes with being JUST MARRIED! (April)

Go back in time and discover the West as it was meant to be . . . UNTAMED— Maverick Hearts! (July)

LINGERING SHADOWS
New York Times bestselling author Penny Jordan brings you her latest blockbuster. Don't miss it! (August)

BACK BY POPULAR DEMAND!!!
Calloway Corners, involving stories of four sisters coping with family, business and romance! (September)

FRIENDS, FAMILIES, LOVERS
Join us for these heartwarming love stories that evoke memories of family and friends. (October)

Capture the magic and romance of Christmas past with HARLEQUIN HISTORICAL CHRISTMAS STORIES! (November)

WATCH FOR FURTHER DETAILS IN ALL HARLEQUIN BOOKS!

CALEND

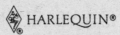

HARLEQUIN®

my Valentine *1993*

The most romantic day of the year is here! Escape into the exquisite world of love with MY VALENTINE 1993. What better way to celebrate Valentine's Day than with this very romantic, sensuous collection of four original short stories, written by some of Harlequin's most popular authors.

ANNE STUART
JUDITH ARNOLD
ANNE McALLISTER
LINDA RANDALL WISDOM

THIS VALENTINE'S DAY, DISCOVER ROMANCE WITH MY VALENTINE 1993

Available in February wherever Harlequin Books are sold.

VAL93

Take 4 bestselling love stories FREE

Plus get a FREE surprise gift!

COME FOR A VISIT—TEXAS-STYLE!

**Where do you find hot Texas nights, smooth Texas charm an[d]
dangerously sexy cowboys? CRYSTAL CREEK!**

This March, join us for a year in Crystal Creek...wher[e]
power and influence live in the land, and in the hands of on[e]
family determined to nourish old Texas fortunes and to forg[e]
new Texas futures.

CRYSTAL CREEK reverberates with the exciting rhythm [of]
Texas. Each story features the rugged individuals who liv[e]
and love in the Lone Star State. And each one ends with th[e]
same invitation...

Y'ALL COME BACK...REAL SOON!

Watch for this exciting saga of a unique Texas family i[n]
March, wherever Harlequin Books are sold.

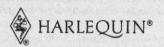

HARLEQUIN®

HAPPY VALENTINE'S DAY

James Rafferty had only forty-eight hours, and he wanted to make the most of them.... Helen Emerson had never had a Valentine's Day like this before!

Celebrate this special day for lovers, with a very special book from American Romance!

#473   ONE MORE VALENTINE
by Anne Stuart

Next month, Anne Stuart and American Romance have a delightful Valentine's Day surprise in store just for you. All the passion, drama—even a touch of mystery—you expect from this award-winning author.

Don't miss American Romance
#473   ONE MORE VALENTINE!

Also look for Anne Stuart's short story, "Saints Alive," in Harlequin's MY VALENTINE 1993 collection.

WELCOME TO

The quintessential small town,
where everyone knows everybody else!

Each book set in Tyler is a self-contained love story; together,
the twelve novels stitch the fabric of the community.

"The small town warmth and friendliness shine through."
Rendezvous

Join your friends in Tyler for the twelfth book,
LOVEKNOT by Marisa Carroll, available in February.

*Does Alyssa Baron really hold the key to Margaret's death?
Will Alyssa and Edward consummate the romance they began more than
thirty years ago?*

GREAT READING...GREAT SAVINGS...AND A
FABULOUS FREE GIFT!

With Tyler you can receive a fabulous gift, ABSOLUTELY FREE,
by collecting proofs-of-purchase found in each Tyler book.
And use our special Tyler coupons to save on your next
TYLER book purchase.

If you missed *Whirlwind* (March), *Bright Hopes* (April), *Wisconsin Wedding* (May), *Monkey Wrench* (June), *Blazing Star* (July), *Sunshine* (August), *Arrowpoint* (September), *Bachelor's Puzzle* (October), *Milky Way* (November), *Crossroads* (December) or *Courthouse Steps* (January) and would like to order them, send your name, address, zip or postal code, along with a check or money order for $3.99 for each book ordered (please do not send cash), plus 75¢ postage and handling ($1.00 in Canada), payable to Harlequin Reader Service, to:

In the U.S.

3010 Walden Avenue
P.O. Box 1325
Buffalo, NY 14269-1325

In Canada

P.O. Box 609
Fort Erie, Ontario
L2A 5X3

Please specify book title(s) with your order.
Canadian residents add applicable federal and provincial taxes.

TYLER-12